Most Wanted

Most Wanted

VIVETTE J. KADY

The Porcupine's Quill

Library and Archives Canada Cataloguing in Publication

Kady, Vivette J., 1954–
Most Wanted/Vivette J. Kady.

Short stories.
ISBN 0-88984-259-0

I. Title.

PS8621.A39M68 2005   C813'.6   C2004-906571-8

Published by The Porcupine's Quill,
68 Main Street, Erin, Ontario NOB 1T0.
www.sentex.net/~pql

Readied for the press by John Metcalf; copy edited by Doris Cowan.

Represented in Canada by the Literary Press Group.
Trade orders are available from University of Toronto Press.

We acknowledge the support of the Ontario Arts Council,
and the Canada Council for the Arts for our publishing program.
The financial support of the Government of Canada
through the Book Publishing Industry Development Program
is also gratefully acknowledged. Thanks, also, to the Government of Ontario
through the Ontario Media Development Corporation's
Ontario Book Initiative.

Canada Council   Conseil des Arts
for the Arts   du Canada

Canadä

ONTARIO ARTS COUNCIL
CONSEIL DES ARTS DE L'ONTARIO

To the memory of my father
and for my mother and Moss and Ruby

TABLE OF CONTENTS

ANYTHING THAT WIGGLES

Early that summer, my grandma dropped dead watching *The Price Is Right*, and the following week Aunt Lois, my mother's sister, moved in and declared we would no longer be running a breeding factory.

'This place is disgusting, Sandra. It stinks,' she told my mother after she'd dragged her suitcases up to my grandma's old bedroom. 'Dog poop under the kitchen table, piddle everywhere you walk. We won't even talk about the yard, which is a total disaster. And what's that piece of mouldy bread doing over by the sofa?' She placed a cool dry hand on the back of my neck. 'You can't raise your daughter in a pigsty.'

A few days later she counted the $450 she got from selling the last of our poodle Antoinette's puppies, then wiped her hands on her pink button-front beautician's smock and announced that the bitch would be spayed and that was that.

My mother winced and hugged her arms across her belly.

'Now don't give me that long face, Sandra,' Aunt Lois said. 'She's already had five litters.'

But bullying our tenant, Roy Steele, into getting rid of the pigeons he kept in our backyard wouldn't be so easy.

'He'll probably die without them,' my mother wailed. 'Don't make him, Lois.'

'He sometimes even talks like a pigeon,' I added.

'Poorrrr poorrrr,' my mother cooed, closing her eyes. 'Poorrrr poorrrr.'

'I had an agreement with your mother,' Roy Steele told Aunt Lois. 'I take care of the yard, and I get to keep my pigeons.'

Roy's voice was soft as a puppy's belly. He stroked his beard and squinted in the sunlight. He was carrying a large plastic No Frills bag, and wearing his usual outfit: a stained grey suit jacket with patched elbows; flip-flops; a waist-length white halter-top blouse; a below-the-knee summer skirt with bunches of tiny white flowers on a background that matched his blue eyes.

'That's right,' my mother nodded fiercely. 'He did, Lois. Mom said he could.'

Roy became my grandma's tenant soon after his wife Bernice died. He must have been about fifty-five or sixty. He had a spongy nose and a sweet face that crumpled when he smiled, and he kept Bernice's ashes in a dog-shaped cookie jar. My grandma used to look out the kitchen window and sigh at the sight of Roy cooing to his pigeons. 'Grief,' she'd say.

'You've got to be joking,' Aunt Lois said. 'Look at the state of this yard.'

'Lawnmower's broke,' Roy told her. 'You get a new lawnmower, I'll cut the grass.'

When Aunt Lois said we were running a breeding factory in my grandma's house, she didn't just mean Antoinette's puppies and Roy's pigeons. She also meant me, because if my mother has any idea who my father is, she's never let on.

'Could be that school teacher down the road, whatsisname, McDougal,' my grandma once said. 'That'll explain where Angie gets her brains. And that man'll go after anything that wiggles.'

Aunt Lois figured my grandma should've had my mother fixed years ago so she couldn't have any babies, because of her affliction. Aunt Lois's eyebrows lifted and her nostrils got wide when she said 'affliction.'

Grandma shrugged and said, 'No matter – a baby brings its own love into the world.'

My mother fell off a dresser onto her head when she was six months old. She does most things slowly – she talks slowly, blinks slowly, laughs five seconds after everyone else. And she has seizures.

'I get lightning storms,' she once told me, 'right inside my head,' and for the longest time after that, whenever my mother's eyes started to flutter and it looked as if she were slipping off into one of her fits, I'd peer up her nostrils, hoping to see the bright jolts that lit up her shocked blue skull.

Aunt Lois decided she was going to quit her job at Top to Toe Beautiful! and open a beauty salon in our house. She figured the basement would be perfect, and counted the advantages on her fingers: 'Separate entrance. Separate bathroom. No rent. Zero travel time to work. Location's not bad – there's a bus stop right around the corner. And I get to be my own boss. Plus, I can keep an eye on things around here.'

My mother shoved a forkful of meat loaf into her mouth. Her calm brown eyes slowly blinked. 'In the basement?'

'Please don't talk with your mouth full, Sandra. It might be a little dark right now, but nothing a few fluorescents and a fresh coat of paint can't fix. It maybe needs a couple pieces of drywall. We'll make it nice.'

My mother chewed and swallowed before she spoke again. 'But Roy lives down there. In the basement.'

'Well, yes, I'm aware of that. And I'm sorry about Roy. But *some*body's got to work around here.'

'We had an agreement, your mother and me,' Roy said quietly. 'Signed. I've got the lease.'

He was sitting very straight in my grandma's favourite armchair, with the knotted No Frills bag on his lap. I tried to guess what he kept in it. Something bulky – maybe the jar with Bernice's ashes. He'd shown me that jar one day, down in his room – a happy-face dog with black spots and a sloppy red tongue. You opened it by twisting the head off.

'Well,' Aunt Lois said, 'you know, circumstances have changed.'

'Hey.' My mother looked up from the spot she'd been staring at on the carpet. Her face had lit up like a soft white moon. She pointed at the ceiling. 'You can live upstairs, Roy.'

'Upstairs.' Aunt Lois's voice was flat.

My mother nodded happily. 'In the attic.'

Aunt Lois sighed and shook her head. 'No, Sandra. There's no way he's living up there. He'd have to share our bathroom.'

Roy scratched his beard. 'That'll be okay.'

'We're all females,' Aunt Lois said.

Roy shifted back in the armchair and crossed his scabbed, hairy legs. 'I don't mind.'

'Well, there's no kitchen up there.'

'I don't like to cook. I'll take it.' His blue eyes creased at the corners. 'Less fifty a month.'

Aunt Lois arranged for her ex-husband's cousin Tony to cover up pipes and ducts, put in some new lights, replace the stained broadloom, and patch and paint the basement.

'He's giving us a good price,' she said. 'And I've got nothing against Tony. *He* can't help it if his cousin's a loser.'

Tony came and went in his blue panel van, carrying tools and drywall and cans of paint. He was big – over six feet, and heavy – but he moved around so quietly you almost forgot he was there until the hammering and drilling started. He didn't say much – 'He's not exactly the sharpest knife on the block,' Aunt Lois said – but that didn't stop my mother hanging around him. She kept bringing him doughnuts and Diet Pepsis.

A couple of days after Tony started on the basement, he arrived as Roy was going out to take care of his pigeons. 'Something wrong with that guy?' Tony asked.

I was holding the side door open while he carried his stuff in.

'No,' I answered. 'He just dresses weird.'

'Yes, there is,' my mother said. She'd come up suddenly behind Tony and he jumped when she spoke. 'Grief.'

'Jeez,' he said, 'you scared me.'

'For his wife. She died.'

'Oh,' Tony said.

'Bernice. She had cancer.' She pushed away some hair from her eyes. 'Want something to eat?'

He shook his head. 'I'm okay. I just got here,' he said, and ducked down the basement stairs.

School had been out for a couple of days when my grandma died. I'd been playing with Antoinette's puppies on the kitchen floor. I could hear the TV in the living room: 'Travis Conway, come on down!'

'Angie!' my mother screamed.

On the TV, Bob Barker was saying, 'Here come my beauties with the next item up for bids.'

My grandma was in her favourite armchair, her head flung back, legs thrust forward.

'It's a new washer and dryer!'

My mother had backed away from my grandma. She stood, rigid, next to the TV. The mute blue-suited blonde woman on the TV screen curtsied and smiled as she caressed the top of the washing machine with long red fingernails. 'Call 911,' my mother said.

I ran to the kitchen, dialled the number, gave the emergency operator details, ran back to the living room. 'He says we have to talk to her until they get here.'

'Mom,' my mother said. She stayed next to the TV set. 'Please, Mom, don't.'

'Actual retail price is $550,' Bob Barker said.

Within minutes, sirens were wailing. I opened the door, and pointed to the living room. Large black-booted paramedics clumped in and swarmed around my grandma's chair.

'And it's a fabulous trip to Denmark!'

The lucky contestant was hopping and shrieking and flapping her arms. My mother rocked back and forth, her hands clawing at the sleeves of her T-shirt.

One of the paramedics took the remote from my grandma's lap and turned off the TV. My mother kept rocking. A thick humming sound pushed past her throat and tongue.

When the basement was ready, delivery men arrived with boxes of beauty supplies and an adjustable esthetician's table. We unpacked lotions and creams, cuticle sticks and cotton balls, and stacked clean folded towels on shelves. Aunt Lois hung her framed beauty school diploma on the wall. On a sheet of blank paper, she carefully wrote:

Esthetic Care by Lois
~ facials ~ manicures ~ pedicures ~ eyebrow & eyelash tinting ~
~ waxing ~ nail extensions ~
Exclusive Professional Service for a New You
Call 245-3063 for an appointment
331 Bartlett Street (side door)

She drew daisies with intertwined stems around the border of the page, then made 500 photocopies on bright pink paper. We shoved the flyers through mail slots, tacked them up in laundromats and supermarkets, and stapled them to hydro poles. Within three days, she'd set up an appointment for her first client.

'A bikini and underarm wax,' she announced triumphantly. 'Now Roy had better get this yard in shape.'

Half an hour before her first client was due to arrive, my mother and I were helping Aunt Lois prepare. We smoothed a crisp blue sheet over the padded beauty table; we set out some powder and Kleenex and cloth strips.

'Listen, both of you,' she said, adjusting the temperature of the melting wax. 'I want to make sure you understand I'm running a business here. Please don't come down while I'm busy with a client.'

Blood flared across my face. 'We wouldn't.'

'Good. I don't mean to hurt your feelings, Sandra. But you'd scare people off if you had one of your fits down here.'

'Yes,' my mother said. But I knew it was an almost unbearable loss, to be excluded from the mysteries of those beautiful bottles with their sweet-scented lotions and masques; the rows of sponges and Q-tips and nail polish; those tidy towels.

Before Aunt Lois's first client could make it to the side door, she was greeted by Antoinette and Roy. Antoinette had darted past Roy when he opened the front door. She bounded up to the visitor, wagging her tail and yapping, then stood up on her hind legs, hugged her forelegs around the woman's skinny calf, and began humping it enthusiastically.

Roy nodded politely. The client gaped at him. She shook her leg, but Antoinette held fast. The poodle's tongue was licking in and out.

'Dog's taken a fancy to you,' Roy said.

'Oh, for Chrissakes,' Aunt Lois hissed from the hallway. 'Angie, go get that stupid animal!'

I ran out and scooped up Antoinette. 'Bad girl!' I scolded. 'Sorry,' I mumbled to the woman.

Roy winked at me, bowed slightly to the woman, and walked off down the street. The woman looked stunned. She rubbed her leg absently.

Tony had fastened a brass sign to the side door: *Esthetics by Lois*. Aunt Lois smiled brightly as she opened the door. 'You must be Celine,' she said. 'This way.'

'The guy with the beard, is he one of those, whatyacallits, crossdressers?' Celine asked as she followed Aunt Lois down the basement steps.

When the appointment was over, Aunt Lois's face was grim. 'In future, when a client comes, stay out of my way,' she said. 'All of you. And lock up that damned dog.'

'Squab,' Roy said. 'That's what the young ones are called. People eat them.'

'Yuck,' I said.

'They do, though. In fancy restaurants. Pay a lot of money for them, too. They're tasty – plump and tender.'

I fake-vomited. Roy smiled. He spread grass clippings over the wood shavings that lined the pigeons' nest boxes.

What I liked best about Roy was that he never asked difficult questions. A whole morning could go by without him once asking what you learned in school, or what you planned to be when you were older, or why you didn't have friends over.

'Hello, Mabel. Hi there, Percy,' he said. 'Are you my beauties? Yes, you are. Poorrrr, poorrrr.'

He put fresh water and pigeon pellets into tin cans. His finger-nails were chewed and dirty, and covered with chipped silver nail polish. The birds inched closer, bandy-legged, their small hard heads pulsing in and out. They blinked their eyes.

'If that makes you throw up, you want to see what the parents feed the babies.'

'Is it really gross?'

He opened his mouth wide and pointed down his throat. 'Pigeon milk. Stuff they make inside their crops.'

I pulled a disgusted face. He looked pleased.

The screen door slammed and my mother came charging towards us.

'I'm going on a date!' she yelped.

'Whoa,' Roy said.

She stood red-faced and breathless. There was a bright blob of jelly at the corner of her mouth. Her smile was pure joy. 'For Chinese food. Tonight, with Tony.'

Tony stood in the entrance hall. He shuffled from foot to foot and smoothed his hair. He looked around at the walls, the ceiling, the baseboards, as if checking for cracks.

'I'll go see if she's ready,' I said, and ran upstairs.

Roy was waiting outside the bathroom door. He rolled his eyes at me. 'I think we need to send in a search party. She must've got lost. I'm dying out here. Hey, Sandra,' he called out, 'you planning to take much longer?'

'How bad do you need to go?' she answered.

I rapped on the door. 'Hurry up, Mom. Tony's already here.'

'Tell him to wait.'

She emerged a few minutes later, cheeks rouged, hair sprayed, eyes lined with baby blue iridescent shadow, lips painted a thick glossy coral. She'd used a generous amount of my grandma's old perfume, and she was clutching a black satin purse with both hands. She thrust her chest out and her chin up. 'Am I pretty?' she asked.

I nodded. 'And you smell good.'

'You look very nice, Sandra,' Roy said.

'Thank you.' She wiggled her shoulders, then reached inside the neck of her dress to adjust her bra strap. Roy darted into the bathroom.

Aunt Lois came upstairs. 'What's taking so long?' she asked. She inspected my mother and frowned. 'Wait a minute. Angie, quick, get me a Kleenex.'

She expertly wiped the excess rouge from my mother's cheeks, then held the tissue to my mother's lips. 'Blot,' she said.

'I don't know why we bother. None of them are worth it,' she muttered as we followed my mother down the stairs. My mother turned and gave a little wave when she opened the front door. Tony's hand crept towards the rustling fabric of her dress and his fingers touched her back as she flounced out the door.

Days went by after their date, and Tony didn't call. My mother became distant, drawn into herself, as if she had curled around a secret. She sighed at magazines and the TV, or she lay on the floor patting Antoinette, who watched her with worried eyes. She sat in the yard, listlessly swatting at insects and staring at the grass. Aunt Lois offered to teach her how to give manicures, and my mother practised with orange sticks and bowls of warm fragrant water, but she still moped.

At night I'd thrash my way out of nightmares and slip into her bed. She'd wind strands of my hair around her fingers and we'd lie there, wordless, until we fell asleep, leaning into one another.

Tony finally called, on a sweltering afternoon, more than a week after their date. The air was so thick and humid you could barely breathe, and I'd put on my swimsuit so I could run through the

sprinkler in the backyard. Roy and my mother were sitting on folding lawn chairs under the lilac tree, and Antoinette panted in the
shade under my mother's chair. Aunt Lois came outside after her
two-thirty eyelash tint.

'Have a seat,' Roy said, standing up. 'I'll get another chair.'

'Thank you, Roy.' There were wet circles under the arms of her
pink smock, and she fanned her face and throat with her hands. 'I've
got an hour between clients. What a scorcher.'

When the phone rang, my mother stood so fast she knocked over
the chair, and Antoinette raced with her into the house, barking at
her heels. She came back outside a few minutes later and crashed
through the sprinkler spray, whooping softly, her arms pin-wheeling.
Antoinette circled her, yapping.

'No need to ask who that was,' Roy said.

My mother stood in the centre of the spray, grinning and gasp-
ing.

'This place is a complete madhouse,' Aunt Lois said.

My mother flopped down in her chair, soaking wet. 'Tony's coming,' she announced.

'You better change out of those wet clothes,' Aunt Lois said.

'No. I'm nice and cool,' my mother said.

'Go on, Sandra. You can see right through that blouse.'

My mother giggled, then covered her mouth with her hand. Aunt
Lois frowned.

'I was going to anyway,' my mother said. 'You don't always have
to tell me what to do.' She stood, haughtily. 'When Tony comes, tell
him to wait,' she called over her shoulder.

Roy cleared his throat. Antoinette came over and began humping his leg.

'Antoinette, stop that!' Aunt Lois said.

Roy uncrossed his legs, bent over and patted Antoinette. She
rolled onto her back, and he slipped his foot out of his sandal and
scratched her belly with his toes. I lay on a towel in the sun, my legs
positioned to catch the cool shiver of water as the sprinkler passed to
and fro.

'It's too hot to be watering the lawn. You'll scorch the grass,' Aunt Lois said.

Roy shrugged.

'He'll break her heart, you know.'

Roy shrugged again. 'Maybe not.'

'They're all the same. Only after one thing.' She drew her mouth into a thin line.

'Well,' Roy said, grinning at her, 'I guess sometimes it's worth it. As I recall, that one thing can be very nice.'

Aunt Lois looked at him for a moment, then laughed. 'Sometimes,' she said. After a while, she said, 'What are you doing, wearing a jacket in this heat? There's a humidex warning and you're sitting out here in that jacket.'

Roy smiled, shyly.

'Go on, take it off. You're making me hot just to look at you.'

He took off the jacket. He had dark hairy armpits under the white sleeveless blouse. He smoothed his skirt over his knees, and folded his pale arms across his chest, and I suddenly decided that the skirt and blouse must have belonged to Bernice.

'Do you have children, Roy?' Aunt Lois asked.

'One. She's an artist, out on Galiano Island. She sent me a card a couple weeks ago. Made it herself.' He closed his eyes for a few moments, then he opened them and said, 'I better go see to my pigeons.'

'Oh, sit a while. They can wait. It's too hot to move.' She sniffed. 'Tell me, Roy, what's so special about those birds of yours?'

He thought for a moment. 'They always come back.'

'They always come back?'

'They'll fly off into the wide blue sky, but they'll come back to you.'

'There's a lot to be said for that, I suppose,' Aunt Lois said. 'Speaking of which, here's Tony.'

I sat up on my towel. Tony walked over and sat down carefully in the chair next to Aunt Lois.

'Do you believe this heat?' she asked him.

'It's pretty warm,' Tony said.

'There's a humidex warning.'

'I heard,' he said.

'You did a good job in the basement. No complaints so far.'

'That's good,' he said.

We all sat in silence until my mother came out. She walked up to us, slowly, in her soft yellow sun-dress. 'Hi, Tony,' she said, and smiled wide. There was something off-centre in her eyes. And then her eyelids fluttered, her mouth twitched, and I was sure I could hear the shift and crackle of the boisterous nerves inside her skull.

'Oh boy,' Roy said, 'she's off again,' and we all rose into the heave of that steamy afternoon.

SOFT SPOT

Nick sits on Aura when the baby cries at night. He straddles her, all one-eighty-plus pounds of him, pinning down her arms, pressing powerful thighs and feet against her skinny flailing legs. She struggles and swears; she tries to bite him; she squirms and whimpers and aims a knee at his naked balls but he holds firm. The baby howls, and Aura jerks and sobs.

It's only supposed to take a few nights. Forty minutes the first time, then thirty or twenty, and by the fourth or fifth night the baby should get the message. But his wailing gets progressively worse until it's an hour-long frantic juddering, and on the fifth night Aura wriggles and heaves and breaks free.

Later, she dreams she can't find the baby. She wakes and she's crawling around the foam mattress, drowning in the dark, hands fumbling like blind fish towards the ceiling. She dreams this, and wakes like this, over and over.

Most of the time it's dark inside. They're in a basement apartment, and Nick keeps the drapes drawn. He slips in and out, glancing sideways, because as far as the welfare people are concerned, only Aura and the baby live here. Sometimes he goes out and doesn't come back for a couple of days.

Aura opens the drapes when Nick's not around. Watches legs go by. Slides the window wide to smell the weather. When the bellowing from the white house across the street gets too loud, a girl – she's maybe twelve, or thirteen – comes out and plays her trumpet on the porch. The girl stands up there with her eyes closed and her shoulders swaying, and blasts away.

Aura sings to the baby, songs she makes up. She dances while she sings, rocking him in her arms and jiggling him. She's a singer-poet, like Courtney Love, and one day she'll blow them all away.

Nick tells her to shut the fuck up, he's trying to sleep.

They hadn't planned on a baby, but even before Aura was pregnant, she'd skim fingertips over Nick's skin and they'd choose names. Swift. Sahara. Homer, Caius, Silver. This was when they were crashing on Nick's brother's floor. Zen, or Zed. Nick vetoed Zed because of that part in *Pulp Fiction*: 'Zed's dead, Baby, Zed's dead.' Jak. Jemima. Lily or Lark.

When two blue lines appeared on the test stick from the drugstore pregnancy kit, Aura pictured a beautiful brown-eyed baby girl with an irresistible smile. She'd carry the baby strapped to her back. It would come on tour with the band Aura was going to get together, and she'd bring it onstage, dressed in incredibly cool clothes, like Courtney Love did with Frances Bean. Tiny fur-lined coat, velvet floppy hat, miniature patent-leather shoes.

Aura examined her changing shape in the cracked bathroom mirror. She knotted her T-shirt beneath her swelling breasts and stroked her expanding belly as she swung her hips in slow circles. She grinned at herself and pouted and licked her lips. She slid a hand under the waistband of her panties as she danced to the music in her head, grinding and pushing faster and faster. Then she threw up.

He's not a beautiful baby. His ears jut out and he gets blotchy rashes. His legs dangle, stick-thin and bandy, or tuck up when he shrieks. He's all appetite and voice; a frenzied, beating thing. He frowns as he pulls at her breast, smacking and sucking, a sour-milk smell steaming off him. His head presses into the crook of her arm and she wonders about the things that bind them – buried, silent things encoded in blood and bone.

Aura's hair is growing out. Dark brown roots; pink and yellow at the ends. She walks around the apartment wearing lilac or lime-green or fuchsia slips, lace-edged and stained. They rustle when she moves, kiss her bruised thighs, slide over her belly and breasts. Make-up smudges under her eyes. Open lipstick tubes and magazines and scraps of paper with scribbled song lyrics litter the floor. She smokes cigarettes down to the filters; forages for butts in the ashtrays. She picks up an old issue of *Spin* but there's no time to read because the baby cries. When she goes to him he palps the air with fists and feet.

The towel rail is on the bathroom floor. She went berserk one night, strung out after some bad dope, and ripped it right off the wall.

Nick draws the baby while it sleeps. He draws Aura nursing the baby. He draws his own feet. He's good. He uses anything he can find to draw with – ballpoint pens, chewed eyeliner pencils, lipstick. He draws on envelopes and flyers. Sometimes he does chalk pictures on downtown sidewalks, and passersby give him money. Aura goes with him when she feels like it. She spreads a blanket on the sidewalk alongside him for her and the baby. Nick gets more money when people see the baby.

Aura hates the gloom inside the basement apartment. She scoops up the baby and takes him out for a walk. She carries him until her arms get tired and her feet hurt, then she finds a bench or some steps to sit on and lays him across her lap. When it's grey or windy they go into the conservatory in the park and sit by the waterfall. She shows him orchids and cacti and his eyes are bright river pebbles.

She goes for hours without eating, and sometimes she goes for days without speaking to anyone.

She passes the white house across the street and the girl on the front porch jeers at some boys going by. The girl plays her trumpet while someone shouts inside the house and things crash against walls. The girl doesn't miss a note. When Aura stares too long, the girl stops playing and gives her the finger, *Fuck you.*

She watches the baby jerk or grimace or suck in his sleep. Dreaming of food, or being twisted from her. When she's stoned, she puts him beside her on the foam mattress and stares at the tip of his tongue moving between his lips. Tiny blue veins on translucent eyelids. Bright blood pulsing under new skin. She falls asleep and when she wakes he's screaming and she's forgotten who she is.

Nick brings them presents. A rubber giraffe for the baby. A McDonald's plastic cup. An old toaster oven. Dope.

One afternoon Aura and the baby come back from a walk and there's a TV in the middle of the floor. She asks Nick where it came from and all he says is, 'Don't worry about it.'

She hates the gloom so she takes the baby and wanders. She walks for hours while he shifts or sleeps in her arms. Sometimes he's so heavy she thinks she'll drop him. He'll slip away, slide from her aching arms.

One rainy day they drift in and out of stores and she shoplifts some powder-blue Hard Candy nail polish. Back in the apartment, she paints the baby's fingernails and toenails and then she paints her own. When she's done, she turns the bottle upside-down to read the name of the colour. 'Sky,' she tells the baby. 'That's a cool name. Maybe we should have called you Sky.'

Nick brings them things: a fold-up garden chair; an old stroller; an Asterix book with a torn cover. Nick and Aura read Asterix together on the mattress, giggling, while the baby sleeps on Nick's chest. When the baby wakes, they prop him up so he's sitting between them, and laugh when he topples over. Aura gives him her great-grandmother's silver bracelet to teethe on. They eat peanut butter sandwiches and watch *Jeopardy* and wish they had cable.

Nick brings a stereo, and Aura won't ask where it came from. Then he doesn't show up for a few days and she worries someone will come looking for him. She keeps the drapes drawn and watches *The Young and the Restless* and *Oprah* with the volume turned low, and wishes she could get high.

The night she left home, with a guy who'd once done time for auto theft, her father said, 'I wash my hands of you.' Her mother

cried. She ran out after Aura, grabbed her wrist and said, 'Please.'
They live a hundred and ten kilometres away and she hasn't seen
them for almost four years. They probably think she spends all day
shooting up in a dark room.

She watches the news, strumming her guitar and singing softly
while houses burn and planes crash, and she wonders if Nick is
bleeding or sick or dead.

When he comes back he tells her it's okay, he just had to take
care of some stuff.

Aura doesn't buy the conspiracy theory bullshit – Courtney Love
had nothing to do with Kurt Cobain's death. Four days after her
band released its second album, her husband put a shotgun to his
head and pulled the trigger. There was enough smack in his blood-
stream to kill him anyway.

Courtney Love called her band Hole because of something her
mother told her: *You can't go walking around with a hole in yourself
just because you had a bad childhood.*

The baby cries at night and Nick rides her thrusting bucking body
and laughs.

One wheel wobbles on the stroller Nick brought, but it's easier than
carrying the baby. She pushes him through parks and alleys and
under bridges, and doesn't speak for hours. She's suspended high
above words; syllables are becoming distant, glinting things. She
feels an unexpected lightness, and a word glides by: *joy*.

One afternoon as she pushes the stroller in front of the white
house across the street, the girl comes out and slams the screen door.
'Suck it up!' she yells over her shoulder. She looks at Aura and Aura
waits for the fuck-you finger but the girl says, 'Oh look, you've got a
baby!' and leaps down the porch steps. She stands grinning in front
of the stroller. 'I love babies. Boy or girl?'

'Boy,' Aura says.

The girl is wearing baggy khaki pants and she's braided strands of hemp and coloured feathers into her hair. She directs a variety of facial expressions and cooing sounds at the baby. 'Hey, he likes me. He's smiling. I'll baby-sit for you. I'm crazy about babies. If you want a break, like, you know, a night on the town –'

Aura laughs. She finds this unbelievably funny – *a night on the town*. The girl seems bewildered. She looks a bit like Aura's kid sister, who's wanted to be an astronaut since she was eight years old and spends every school holiday at a camp for science geeks. Or maybe she no longer wants to be an astronaut, because she must be sixteen already, and their mother is probably finding bras between the couch cushions and money missing from her purse.

Aura stops laughing. 'Sure.' She smiles at the girl. 'Thanks.'

When Aura and the baby get back a couple of hours later, the girl waves from the front porch. 'Hey, wait up!' she shouts. She dashes into her house for a moment, then runs across the street carrying some plastic shopping bags. 'My mom says you can have these. We don't need them any more.'

Aura looks inside the bags: baby clothes, a crocheted yellow blanket, a purple stuffed elephant, a rattle. She opens her mouth but words slip by, wafer-thin.

The girl takes the rattle from the bag, shakes it, then hands it to the baby. He puts it in his mouth. 'I gotta go,' she says. 'Bye-bye baby.'

Aura gives Nick a box of pastels for his birthday. He brings a bottle of tequila and some doughnuts. He's bummed because it's his birthday and all he's managed to score is some hash. She sings 'Happy Birthday' and he blows out the candle she shoved into a chocolate doughnut. He tells her he wishes he'd be discovered by a famous art critic.

'You shouldn't have told,' she says. 'Now it won't come true.'

Nick says maybe they should move someplace warm. Winter's coming, and you can't draw on sidewalks when there's snow. Aura lets the baby suck her chocolatey finger, and says she won't squat freezing warehouses or sleep on park benches or in all-night coffee shops, never again.

Nick tries out his new pastels on the wall behind the mattress. He draws a mural of a beautiful woman leaning out a yellow window, and under the window is a grinning crocodile wearing a suit. The woman has black hair and scarlet lips and she looks bored. Aura worries about the landlord, but Nick tells her to chill, it'll wash off.

They finish the tequila and when she wakes it's daylight and the room blurs and spins. Nick's not there and she's forgetting something. Then she realizes the baby's gone too.

She sees them outside the 7-Eleven as she turns the corner: Nick with his hands in his windbreaker pockets, shivering; the baby's head bobbing slightly in his stroller, his eyes flaming. Nick is panhandling, telling passersby he needs to buy milk for the baby. A child tugs at her mother's jeans, and the mother rummages in her purse for change. The child hands the money to Nick and the baby smiles. An older woman walks by and shouts at Nick. She gave him enough money for milk twenty minutes ago. Why won't he take the baby home and feed it? Then Nick sees Aura but he doesn't move. Her stomach twists and she turns around and heads back to the apartment. She lies on her side underneath the grinning crocodile and the bored woman, and hugs her knees. She feels numb.

Nick brings the baby back half an hour later.

'Asshole,' she hisses.

The baby teethes and drools on the giraffe's rubber neck. Aura writes songs. She doesn't want to be like Courtney Love any more. She'd never have plastic surgery, or shop at Versace, but someday she'll be on the cover of *Rolling Stone*.

One day she goes out walking with the baby and when they get back the stereo's gone. She's in the bathroom when Nick comes home, filling the basin with water and balancing the naked baby on her hip. Nick's out of his head, but when he holds out his arms she gives him the baby. He rubs the baby's back and kisses him. Aura tests the water with her wrist, turns back to take the baby and sees Nick sway. She sees the baby slip through his arms and she's reaching out but not fast enough. The little naked body arcs over and falls, head first, and she can't catch him although it takes so long for him to reach the floor, and there's the unbelievable thud of his head on tile and then dead quiet until he finally screams.

And Nick is holding his hands up in front of his face, shaking his head as if he has water in one ear, and the baby is the only one able to cry.

The girl from across the street says, 'Hey, little guy, what's up?'

Aura takes a deep breath. 'He had a bad fall a couple days ago. He fell on his head.' She has no idea why she's saying this. She can't remember when last she strung so many words together. Her voice sounds thin and her tongue feels swollen.

The girl gapes at her.

Aura says, 'His father dropped him. It was an accident. He didn't mean to.' She thinks, *Now she hates me.*

The girl sighs. She squats on the sidewalk and takes hold of the baby's feet. After a few minutes she says, 'One time when I was five I thought my mother was dead.' She looks at the baby's feet when she says this. 'She was lying in the middle of the floor and my little brothers were shaking her and poking her and she didn't move. When I picked up her arm it just flopped back down, so I called 911 and told them she was dead.' She swings the baby's feet one at a time, up and down, up and down. She draws them apart, then brings them together. Open. Closed. Open. Closed. Then she looks up at Aura. 'He's going to be okay, right?'

'We don't know. He's okay now, but the doctor says there could be problems later. Sometimes it takes years before you find out there's damage.' Aura looks for a cigarette, lights it, exhales. 'Because babies have these soft spots, you know. On their heads.'

The girl says, 'I know.'

Nick hasn't come home for over a week but there's the smell of him on the pillow and his T-shirt's still balled up under the sink. The crocodile and the woman over her mattress are smudged. There are times when she hears the baby but feels too heavy to move, and then he cries until he drags her from sleep.

Nick hasn't come back since the day he dropped the baby, and when the baby fusses Aura jiggles him and pats his back and whispers, 'Hush.' Once or twice she pats too hard, or puts him down too roughly, or gives him a little impatient shake so that he stares at her, stunned, then gasps and howls. She holds him and shivers and remembers how Nick sat on her when he cried at night, and what would she have done to the shuddering rag-doll body if he hadn't? She holds him close, kisses soft downy scalp where bone has not yet fused; she nuzzles the small shell whorls in his ears and whispers, 'I'll get you a better life.'

Someday she'll be under coloured spotlights, the audience roaring, arms waving high, their lighters blazing like floating stars, and she'll dive right off the edge, she'll fly over the surge of outstretched hands.

She smokes cigarettes down to the filters and wishes she could get high and thinks, *He's not coming back, not ever.* She hugs the baby and says, 'You can't count on anyone in this life.'

When she closes her eyes Nick is lurching with the baby, he's blacking out, and she can't forget that slow flip, the baby dropping headlong, the sickening crack of head on floor and how long it takes until he cries. Nick swaying, shaking his head, not remembering, but she'll never shake it away. He hit the ground, bounced, landed on his back. That slow headlong tumble, endlessly replayed. That thud. She puts her hands over her ears, squeezes her eyelids tight, Christ, her baby falling like that. The heart-stopping moment of no sound, until breath returns and the crying starts.

Across the street the girl stands on her porch and the trumpet takes her breath and flings it wide.

DETOUR

The month after he got out of rehab, Frank made a hundred-and-ten-mile detour on his way to his brother's wedding. He first drove an hour south to see the Francis Bacon exhibition, then headed north-east so he could pick up the interstate. He hadn't planned this beforehand. He'd already been driving for about fifteen minutes when he remembered that the exhibition – Bacon's Popes – would be closing soon, so he took the first exit and looped south.

He stood in the gallery, surrounded by screaming popes, and what struck him most was the lack of violence in the paint application. He'd expected fierce, explosive brushstrokes, but from up close the paintings were very controlled, almost subdued.

When he got back into his car, he thought that he should probably find a phone and call to let Rob, his brother, know he'd be late, but he decided not to bother. The wedding wasn't until the following afternoon. He pushed an old Ry Cooder cassette into the tape deck, and as he drove he thought about what he would tell Rain, the woman his brother was marrying, about the Bacon exhibition. *Masterful technique,* he would say. *Stand right in front of a painting and you can't make it out, it's just colours. But move back six feet and the eyes jump out at you.*

Ry Cooder was singing, 'Little sister won't you please, please, please....'

The popes look as if their bones are dissolving, he would say. *They're raising fists, or cowering, or shouting dogma. But they're blurred, pulpy, evaporating.*

Frank drummed the steering wheel and sang along, 'Little sister don't you kiss me once and twice, say it's very nice and then you ru-u-un, woo woo woo woo....'

Most days I feel like those popes, he would say. *Like I could just open my mouth and howl.*

He tried to conjure up Rain's face, but all he came up with was the image of a lockjawed pope. Rob and Rain. Christ, the alliteration should've been enough to get them to call off the wedding.

He turned up the volume on the tape deck and rolled down the window. He liked driving. He'd be happy to go on doing it, day after day, criss-crossing the continent and watching the miles unravel. Washing in gas station restrooms; drinking coffee from styrofoam cups; pulling over on back roads and reclining the seat when he needed sleep. He liked the shift in perspective that came with speed: the funnelled pull of the road; that swift freefall through landscape until he became the stationary point, the still centre, while trees and buildings and signs hurtled past.

Going to this wedding was Frank's biggest test since rehab. It was one of the hardest things he'd ever had to do. Maybe he and Rob would pummel one another in the middle of the ceremony with that fierce, murderous fury peculiar to brothers. 'Are you okay with this?' Rob had asked when he called to say he was getting married, and Frank knew that whatever answer he gave, it wouldn't make a bit of difference. That's how it was with Rain.

You know how you look at something and suddenly it all makes sense, he could tell her. *It's like God comes down for a moment.*

And then she'd smile that crooked, wicked, moist-lipped grin that made his knees collapse.

I'm still crazy in love with you, he could say. *Marry me instead.*

A half-hour from his brother's place, Frank broke into a sweat. No telling what he might do, but he was pretty sure it was going to be something stupid. He pulled over at a gas station, filled the tank, and bought a Coke, a pack of Marlboros and some gum. In the men's room, he splashed water over his face and hair, changed his T-shirt, and realized he was definitely planning to win Rain back.

He hadn't seen her for twenty years, but he'd never stopped loving her. Not even while he was married. Anna, his wife, left him the night (or early morning, technically) he smashed the Honda into a parked car a few blocks from their house. The cops had found him walking down the road, totally naked but unhurt, a couple of doors from home. He tried to explain to the police, and later to Anna, that he was naked because there was a hot tub at the party. The party was full of *industry types*, he kept saying. Movie pricks so thick you tripped over them. '*Vanity Fair* wants me to photograph Tarantino,' he told them, but nobody cared.

'You just *consume* everything,' Anna had said when he tried to stop her from leaving. 'Whatever it is, you'll keep on and on until it's all used up. Drugs, booze, love, everything.'

That was six months ago, but it had been a long time coming.

Rain was an art student named Sharon Riley when Frank fell in love with her. Sharon reinvented herself as Rain – legally, with new ID – back when people were still naming themselves or their children after celestial bodies, or seasons, or various expanses of water.

'Why *rain?*' Frank had asked, running a finger down her beautiful spine. 'Rain's such a bummer. It's cold and wet and nasty.'

'No, not *that* kind,' she'd said, her voice muffled by the pillow. 'The gentle kind. Soft and misty.'

'Ah,' he said. 'Drizzle.'

They spent two years together, then she left him for a diamond cutter. The day she packed her bags, they sat on the bed for a while. Whenever he tried to say something, she shook her head and brushed her fingers over his mouth. 'I'm not changing my mind,' she said.

And now he couldn't even picture her face. Every time he closed his eyes, all he could see was a screaming pope.

It was evening when Frank pulled up outside his brother's house. He figured the Escort parked in the driveway had to belong to his mother – the vanity plates read BI Z B. He turned off the ignition, leaned back and shut his eyes. He stayed like that for ten or maybe twenty minutes, every vein in his body pulsing, until there was a rap on the side of the car.

'Frank?' Rob's smile was uncertain, as if he thought Frank might be someone else.

'Shit,' Frank said. 'You gave me a heart attack.'

'You okay? We were getting a little concerned.'

'I'm fine. Took a bit of a detour.'

'You just sitting here?'

'I was about to come in.' Frank got out of the car and pointed at the Escort. 'Mom's here?'

'Uh-huh. In full force.'

'Running around like a blue-assed fly?'

'Absolutely.'

Frank shook his head. 'Busy bee? Shit. What the hell was she thinking?'

Rob grinned and slapped an arm around Frank's back. 'Hey. It's good to see you.'

'Likewise.'

He squeezed Frank's shoulder. 'It means a lot to us. Really.'

Frank removed his bag, his camera equipment and the wedding present from the trunk. He'd bought a large, asymmetrical copper vase, and immediately regretted the purchase. It cost too much and looked as if it had been flung against a wall numerous times. The woman in the store had gift-wrapped it really nicely, though. She'd sprinkled a handful of small silver stars inside the box, and then she'd curled thin strands of pale green and black ribbon around it. He wasn't going to return the vase once she'd gone to so much trouble.

'Here,' Frank handed Rob the gift. 'This is for you.' He lit a Marlboro. His hands were trembling. 'Where's Rain?'

'Gone to pick up the flowers. She'll be back soon. Please don't smoke inside, okay?'

Frank exhaled slowly. 'Okay.' He took a few more drags on the Marlboro, then flicked it under a shrub. His brother had a nice garden, and a nice house in a secluded neighbourhood. He was a partner in a law office.

'Mom?' Rob called as he ushered Frank indoors. 'Look who I found.'

Their mother appeared at the kitchen door. 'Oh, Frank.' She

wiped soapy hands on her apron. She was huffing from all the running around. 'You made it.'

'Hi, Mom,' Frank said, and kissed her. She was plump and soft and she smelled like an odd mixture of vanilla and onions.

'We were worried.' She flapped her hand in front of her nose and frowned. 'You're smoking again?'

Frank shrugged. 'One thing at a time.'

'Cut him some slack, Mom,' Rob said. 'He just got here.'

'We expected you hours ago,' she said.

'I was delayed. Nice car.'

She looked confused.

'The Escort? Outside?' Frank said.

'Is that how long since you were here? That's the car Rob bought me. Isn't it wonderful?'

'Gorgeous,' Frank said. He desperately needed to put something into his mouth. 'Got any coffee?'

'I'll make some,' Rob said. He patted Frank's stomach, which was newly toned after weeks of obsessive post-rehab sit-ups. 'You're looking good. Doesn't he look good? There's a towel in the bathroom if you want to take a shower or anything.'

Frank sniffed under his arms. 'I'm okay.'

'Now, Frank,' their mother lowered her voice and gave him a worried look when Rob went into the kitchen. 'You're not going to cause any trouble, are you?'

He felt the heat spread over his face. 'Come on, give me some credit.'

She sighed. 'Because it's going to be such a nice wedding. Everything's running smoothly.'

'That's good,' he said.

'Although I wonder if Rob has any idea what he's getting into.' Her mouth tightened. 'That girl is *not* easy.'

'Rain?'

'Oh, Rain's no angel. But that daughter of hers is impossible.'

She might as well have swatted Frank right off his feet. His breath caught in his throat. 'She has a daughter?'

'You didn't know? Two children. A girl and a boy.'

Frank felt suddenly old, and sadder than he'd been in years. Until this moment, he'd somehow believed that Rain would still be the same as she was the day he last saw her.

'She stole her mother's car this morning. Right in the middle of everything, she decides to go on a little joyride. That girl needs a good whack on the you-know-what.' She cleared her throat and muttered, 'Speak of the devil.'

Frank turned around. A kid clomped toward him in killer platform shoes. She looked nine or ten at the most, but her bleached hair was cropped short to reveal multiple ear piercings, and she was wearing a couple of flimsy tank tops and a slinky skirt that had a thigh-high slit on one side. Her eyes were rimmed with glittery blue, her lips were glossed silver, and she was scowling.

'Molly,' his mother said, 'this is Frank. My other son.'

'Wow.' Frank blinked. He didn't know whether to pat her head or shake her hand. 'Molly? Well. Hi there.' He wondered how a kid that small could see over the steering wheel. And even with those monster platforms, how could she reach the pedals?

She hooked her thumbs in the waistband of her skirt, thrust her hips forward and stared at him. 'I'm not a little kid, I'm fourteen,' she announced in a bored, flat voice. 'I'm small for my age.'

'Oh,' he said. He was smiling and frowning at the same time. 'So. You're Rain's daughter.' He tried to figure out which parts of her looked like Rain. Something about the eyes. And the chin, definitely.

Irritation flickered across her face. She turned to Frank's mother. 'When are we gonna eat?'

Frank's mother took a deep breath. 'Soon,' she said. 'Aren't you looking after your brother?'

Molly shrugged. 'He's watching TV.'

'There's plenty to do around here if you're bored, young lady.'

Molly rolled her eyes.

'Coffee's ready,' Rob called.

'Well, I'll get busy again,' his mother said, and headed back to the kitchen.

Molly opened her mouth wide, stuck out her silver-studded tongue and waggled it at his mother's retreating back. Frank grinned. 'So,' Molly said, fixing her blue-rimmed gaze on him. 'How was rehab?'

'Excuse me?'

Molly glanced sideways and sighed dramatically. 'Oh great,' she muttered. 'The bitch is back.' She stomped off, and Frank saw that the front door was open, and Rain had come in.

She was carrying a bucket of flowers. 'Ohmygod,' she said. 'Frank.'

'Hey, Rain.' His jaw shook when he smiled. 'You look great,' he said, and meant it. Her face had loosened, become softer and sadder, but she was still beautiful.

Rain put down the flowers and hugged him, carefully. Frank's heart slugged and thumped. Then she opened her arms, slid sideways from his grasp and jerked a thumb at the door. 'Help me bring in the flowers?'

Frank was having his third after-dinner coffee. He drank it quickly, because he needed another cigarette. 'The popes obsessed Bacon for years,' he said. 'Every time he finished another one, he thought he still hadn't got it right. He said he was trying to perfect the representation of the human cry.' He'd rehearsed this earlier, in the car, but the only person who seemed remotely interested was Molly. Her eyebrows rose briefly, then plunged into a frown.

They were folding napkins and making centrepieces. Frank's mother had brought over a Martha Stewart magazine. Cardboard, florist's wire, blue metallic paper and flowers littered the living-room floor. Dash, Rain's son, was supposed to fill bowls with candied almonds, but he kept shoving them in his mouth or dropping them, and those that eventually ended up in the bowls were sticky and covered in carpet fibres. Dash was a tiny, semi-toothless, bulbous-kneed six-year-old with a thin face, dark eyes, and skin like speckled eggshell. Frank thought he didn't look much like a kid at all – he looked like a miniature optometrist from New Jersey.

'There's enough misery in the world,' Frank's mother announced. 'I don't need to see paintings of it.'

'Who is this guy?' Rob asked.

'Francis Bacon?' Rain said. 'You know – all those triptychs? He painted mangled torsos. And people who look as if they've been smeared across the canvas by a bus or something.'

She sat cross-legged on the floor. She was barefoot and tanned and her dress had thin straps that kept sliding off her shoulders. Frank's jaw clenched and his knee jiggled. He wanted to reach over and hook his finger under a strap.

Rob shook his head. 'Nope. Doesn't ring a bell.'

'Well,' she said. 'You're not missing much. It's pretty bleak stuff.'

'That's not a centrepiece,' Frank's mother said, frowning at Molly. Molly ignored her. She was hunched over, bending and twisting wire into what seemed to be stick figures in pornographic poses.

Rain looked up. 'Not bad, Molly.'

'She's artistically gifted, like her mother,' Rob said.

Molly held up two figures intertwined in an impossibly athletic coupling. Her expression was blank. 'They're for on top of the wedding cake.'

Frank's mother clucked her tongue and muttered to herself.

'Where's cake?' Dash asked.

'Tomorrow,' Rob said. 'Cake's tomorrow.'

Dash tugged at Frank's T-shirt. He'd had enough of the almonds. 'Wanna play cards?'

'Maybe. Which game?'

'Go Fish!'

'I don't know that one.'

Dash blinked at him, disbelieving, his translucent eyelids veined bluish. 'Come,' he said with a slow smile, and tugged harder.

'Tell you what,' Frank said. 'I'll go have a cigarette, then we'll play.'

Molly looked up from her wire figures. 'Watch out,' she warned. 'He cheats.'

Frank sat outside and smoked. He tilted his head back and blew smoke rings, and when he squinted it looked as if they were lassoing stars. In the morning a party supply truck would drive up and offload tables and chairs and a tent, and this place would be transformed. He would help spread starched white tablecloths and carry boxes of booze (*No problem*, he would say to Rob, *I can handle it*) and wipe dusty tumblers. What the hell had he been thinking? That he was so irresistible she'd stop making centrepieces while he swept her off her feet? And then there she was, her bare feet padding so quietly he felt the air move before he heard her.

'How're you doing, Frank?' she said softly.

'I'm okay,' he said. 'How about you?'

She sat beside him, curved like a comma, her hair falling forward. Her strap had slipped down again. He pushed it back over her shoulder, his fingers lingering for a moment. *Happiness is* this *close*, he could whisper, rolling the strap between thumb and forefinger.

She straightened her back, shifted her shoulders and smoothed her dress over her knees. 'Thanks,' she said. 'Can I have some of that?' She held out her hand for his cigarette.

He fumbled for the pack. 'Here, you want one?'

She shook her head. 'I don't smoke any more.' She plucked the cigarette from his fingers, inhaled deeply and coughed. 'It's a beautiful night,' she said when she'd stopped coughing.

Frank cleared his throat and tried to think of something to say. After a while, he said, 'Dash is a funny little guy, isn't he? Kind of – *old*, you know? He doesn't talk a whole lot, but you get the feeling he knows exactly what's going on.'

'Dash? He's always been like that. He's a wise old soul.'

'Interesting kid. They both are. Molly's a lot like you. Feisty. And smart.'

She gave a little laugh that sounded like a hiccup. 'She'd be mortified if she heard that. She hates me.'

'She's supposed to. She's a teenager.'

'Oh, I don't know. She's really angry. She wants to go back to Michigan.'

'To *Michigan?* You're kidding. Why?'

She smiled her slow, lopsided grin. 'Come on, you've never been there. It's not that bad. She's missing her friends and everything.'

'Actually, I have. I once did a photo shoot in Ypsilanti.'

'Yeah? It's nice around there.'

'It's okay.' He lit another cigarette. 'So why doesn't she go back and live with her father for a while or something?'

'He's dead.'

'Shit,' Frank said. 'I'm really sorry. I had no idea.'

She nodded. 'Last September.'

'The diamond cutter?'

'The what? Oh, no. God. I'd forgotten about him. No. That didn't last.' She looked up at the stars for a while, then she turned to him. 'How do you *do* that – the smoke rings? They're perfect.'

He passed her the cigarette. 'Pretend you're a fish.'

'It's like skipping stones. I could never get it right.' She inhaled, contracted her lips, puffed out smoke. 'See? Useless.' After a few moments she said, 'He killed himself. Gary, my husband. One afternoon he drove out to this lake where his family always rented a cabin and he drowned himself.' Her voice was low and slow.

Frank's mouth was dry. 'Could have been an accident.'

She shook her head. 'No.'

When she stood up a couple of minutes later, she said, 'Your brother's a good guy, Frank. A really decent, solid guy.'

Frank slept at his mother's house that night. He lay in the dark in his old bedroom and thought about the way he'd held Rain in his heart all those years, and how he knew nothing about her. He couldn't remember if she'd always been such a mystery to him. He didn't know what happened to love, or how it got used up, or what made people restless, or why they kept hurting themselves. He thought of the way some lives unfolded like long, empty roads, and he wondered what terrible kind of loneliness could make a man gaze out at the deep middle of a familiar lake one afternoon and calculate the weight it would take to sink down and hold himself beneath its skin.

They held the ceremony in the back garden. Frank handed Rob the wedding ring, and stood by as his brother slipped it on Rain's finger, pulled her close and kissed her.

When it was over, Frank took photographs. He took pictures of Rob and Rain, who mugged for the camera, and he took pictures of his mother, who squeezed his arm and told him how pleased she was that everything was turning out so well. He photographed Molly, who was sullen at first, but became animated after she'd downed a few glasses of champagne, and stuck out her tongue for a close-up. He photographed Dash's sweet gap-toothed grin as he crawled out from under a table, and he photographed a couple of bemused guests examining the wedding cake, which was crowned by Molly's wire creation. He took photographs of the buffet table, and later of people jostling in line and pouncing on the food.

He made small talk with distant relatives and acquaintances he hadn't seen in years, and he gave a speech, a toast to the bride and groom, in which he mentioned that he'd known Rain for a long time. He made a crack about how he'd tested the waters for his little brother, and how pleased he was that Rob had obviously inherited his excellent taste. He went on to say what a good guy his brother was, and how fortunate Rob and Rain were to have found one another. His mother dabbed her eyes as she raised her glass, and Frank recalled that Rob had been his best man when he married Anna eight years ago, but Frank didn't remember much of that wedding because he'd been pretty much out of it the whole time. He did recall that at some point he'd unwrapped wedding gifts and attempted to auction them to the assembled guests, who'd howled with laughter as Anna, shaking her head and grinning, led him away.

He sat beside his mother while they ate, and she cupped her hand over his on top of the table. 'I wish you'd visit more often,' she said, and Frank looked down at her hand and was shocked to see how she'd suddenly aged.

Rob and Rain had hired an R&B band. Frank sipped a Coke while he listened to them play and watched people dance. The band was surprisingly good. Then Rain grabbed the microphone from the vocalist and belted out something bluesy and sweet. Her hips gyrated and her shoulders swayed and she was mesmerizing. He had no idea she could sing like that. When she finished, everyone cheered and clapped and Rob stood there with a delirious grin on his face, unable to take his eyes off her.

The music was loud and people were shouting and laughing. Everyone looked happy in a jagged, frantic kind of way. Frank chewed the ice at the bottom of his glass and thought of Anna again. Anna used to say she was allergic to parties. Mysterious ailments would surface at the last minute – earaches, toothaches, rashes – so she didn't have to go. The night they first met, at a gallery opening, she'd stood alone, fingering the necklace around her long throat and looking miserable. He'd approached her by asking, 'Did somebody die or is it the art?' and her sudden smile was like a door flung wide. 'Party catatonia,' she'd replied. It surprised him how much he wanted Anna to be there at that moment. He decided he'd go inside and call her. He'd tell her he was calling in the middle of his brother's wedding reception. He went into the house and found a phone in the master bedroom. He wondered if he had the right number – he couldn't remember when last he'd called. He hoped she wasn't going to cry, or hang up on him. As he dialled the number, he panicked that some guy might answer. After six rings he got her answering machine. Her voice sounded upbeat, encouraging, but he hung up without leaving a message.

Rain cornered him as he came out of the bedroom. She was flushed and her eyes sparkled. 'Ah, there you are,' she said. 'We need to take some pictures of you.'

'Forget it,' he said. 'I hate being photographed.'

'Oh, come on,' she said, and steered him out of the house. 'There are no pictures of you anywhere. Twenty years from now we'll look at the albums and wonder where the hell you were.'

She recruited Molly to take the pictures – 'She has a great eye,'

Rain said – and Frank obediently put his arm around Rain, and then his brother, and then his mother, and smiled for the camera.

When Rain was satisfied that Molly had taken enough photographs of him, Frank walked around to the front of the house. He thought that it was almost over; all he needed was to get through that night, and in the morning he would head home. He stood in the street and lit a cigarette. He would try Anna's number again, later on, from his mother's house. And then he thought that there was no need to wait until morning. He could leave right away, drive through the night, and get there before the sun came up. He felt exhilarated. He hadn't been this happy in a long while. He heard the distant laughter and music and felt as if he were already miles away, the long road unfurling in his headlights.

DISTANCE

Lester Minty had a reptile grin and eyes that narrowed and winked as if the world were a vast pool hall. His was the kind of face adults wanted to smack, but we kids liked him.

His sister was in the same class as Lester and I, although she was a year older and half a head taller. This was her second attempt at seventh grade. Whereas everything about Lester seemed to be on the verge of breaking loose at any moment – spiky hair veered off his head in all directions and he moved with a bandy-legged swagger – everything about Shirley Minty drooped, as if the constant yank of gravity were too much for her. Her shoulders slumped, her arms dangled, her cheeks and eyelids sagged, her knees bent.

'That girl's ugly as a dog's ass,' my father once said, but he was drunk at the time. Shirley Minty wasn't ugly; it was just that she slouched around like a stunned ventriloquist's dummy, a long thread of drool sliding down her lip. She'd stand duck-footed and alone in the schoolyard, frowning and blinking slowly at the sky as if she were surprised to find herself awake, her brown eyes brimming with moist, unfocused yearning.

My father and I were newcomers to the neighbourhood. One moonless night the previous spring, my mother had slipped away with Ronald Apt's father, leaving a brief and breathless note on the kitchen table.

'That son of a bitch!' my father cursed, and sprinted to the sidewalk. When he came back inside, he reread the note, crumpled it and hurled it against the window. 'Ah, Christ,' he muttered. 'Goddamn PTA.' Mr Apt had been chairman, my mother treasurer.

'She'll be back,' my father predicted, nodding to reassure himself. 'All her things are here.'

When it became clear that she wouldn't, he quit his job, sold the house and all our furniture, and signed on to manage a hardware store a thousand miles away. The evening before we left, he made a large bonfire in the backyard and we stood out there and watched as it burned whatever remnants we held of my mother. With a wild look in his eyes and a flick of his wrist, my father sent her zebra-print pill-box hat sailing like a Frisbee towards the blaze. 'Bull's-eye!' he shouted as it caught fire. Red stilettos and a floral muumuu were next. My father slowly fingered the loose skin beneath his chin. 'There was a time,' he said after a while, his voice full of tired calm, 'I would have set my hair on fire for that woman.'

Ash and smoke drifted across the darkening sky while we waited for the fire to wear itself out. I realized I'd kept nothing back from the flames – not a single keepsake or lucky charm. Then my thoughts sidled away from my mother and I found myself longing for a lace-edged blue gingham bra of my own and the breasts to fill it.

We rented a two-bedroom furnished bungalow three doors away from the Mintys. The upholstery was worn, the wallpaper was peeling, the carpet was pocked with cigarette burns and the house had a wet-sock smell that never went away. The first thing my father did when we moved in was walk through the entire place without saying a word. He opened windows, checked closets, bounced on loose floorboards, tapped walls. He ran his fingers across discoloured patches and sighed deeply. Then he went outside and slowly circled the exterior. 'Okay,' he said when he was done. He patted my shoulder a few times, carefully, as if it might have dry rot. 'Life's not all apples and roses. Let's get unpacked.'

A couple of hours later, I sat with my bare knees hugged against my chest on a concrete step outside the front door. It was still summer, but the weather had been cool and damp all day. I looked around at the hopeless weed-clogged yard and the dreary street, each house on it as tired-looking and bland as the next, and I worried about how my mother was ever going to find us there. That's when I first encountered Shirley Minty. She came slack-limbed along the sidewalk and into the yard, planted her turned-out feet on a cracked paving stone, clasped her hands behind her back and blinked at me. Her eyelids were glossed with brilliant turquoise shadow, and when she blinked the effect was startling. She wore a loose dress made from some sort of clingy fabric, her legs were scabbed and blotchy and her socks flopped around her ankles.

'You get piles,' she finally announced, lisping slightly, 'if you sit like that.'

It took me some time to gather my wits enough to reply. 'What?'

She sniffed loudly and wiped away the dribble that had pooled on her fat lower lip. 'Piles,' she repeated evenly. 'From the cold. My brother's got them. He says it's like shitting razor blades.'

I couldn't think of anything to say, so I released my knees and shifted position. I stretched out my legs and sat on my hands. She watched me for a few moments, her expression placid, then she shrugged, blinked a couple of times, turned around and walked away.

Within half an hour, I met Lester. I was on the sidewalk, squinting at the bungalow, trying to picture how much better it would look with the bricks plastered over and painted mauve with a plum trim and maybe some shutters and a picket fence and a whole new garden, when he strutted by. His hands were in his pockets and his shoulders rolled as he walked. He smiled. I smiled back. He stopped alongside me and looked me over as he rocked slowly back and forth on his heels, grinning all the while.

He said, 'You just move in?'

'Uh-huh. Today.'

He nodded. His eyes crinkled at the corners and they were green and bright as marbles. I ground the toes of one foot into the sidewalk. He kept nodding. 'What grade you in?' he asked. I told him. He said, 'Same here.' He told me he lived down the street, just a couple of houses away, and jerked his head in the direction of his house. I looked over and saw Shirley Minty out there on the sidewalk, watching us. When she realized we'd seen her, she lifted her hand half-heartedly as if she'd been about to catch something and then thought better of it. Her hand flopped down.

'That girl's not normal,' I said.

'Her? Yeah. She's a weirdo.' Lester crossed his green eyes and his index finger made a crazy-person spiral at his temple.

Shirley stood there looking as if she'd been stuck by a pin and deflated. Everything about her was limp. She straightened momentarily and yelled, 'Lester! Dinner's ready,' then she went limp again.

'Sick freak thinks she's my sister,' Lester said. 'They're supposed to keep her locked away.'

'Really?'

He grinned. 'Nah.'

I blushed. My father came outside. 'Hi there,' he said.

I said, 'Hi.' Lester didn't say anything.

My father looked at Lester for a moment, then he turned to me. 'You interested in getting some takeout?'

'Yeah. Noodles?'

'Sure,' my father said.

'See you 'round,' Lester told me. My father and I watched him walk back to his house. Shirley was still out there, waiting. She followed him inside. My father scowled and shook his head. 'I don't like that boy's face,' he said.

My father came into my room that night and sat on the edge of the bed. 'You all set in here?' he asked.

'I guess,' I said.

He glanced over at the trophies I'd won running – 100 metres, 200 metres, relays. They were lined up on top of the dresser.

'I'll rig up a shelf for those,' he said.

'Thanks.'

He lifted a flap of loose wallpaper alongside the bed, then smoothed it down. 'It'll be easier when school starts.'

I nodded.

'You'll make new friends.'

'I know.' I examined my fingernails. They were filthy. 'I don't care that we left.'

He cleared his throat. 'Right.'

After he kissed me goodnight, his breath full of whisky, my

father smiled sadly and said, 'You're nothing like your mother,' and I couldn't tell if he was glad or sorry.

Mrs Minty was a wiry, sharp-faced nurse with peroxided hair and the deepest suntan I ever saw. She worked a lot of night shifts, and on warm sunny days she lay outside for hours in a silver bikini, slathered in baby oil and stretched out on a plastic recliner that left thick red stripes bitten into her back when she flipped over. She chain-smoked and leafed through *True Romance* magazines or her husband's old *Playboy*s, squinting from the glare and the smoke and looking as if she wanted to hurt somebody.

'Oh, that's nice. You found a little friend,' she said to Shirley the first time I went to their house. She had a smoker's wrecked voice and rasping cough. She closed the *Playboy* and tried to hide it under her oiled legs, then she shaded her eyes with one hand and squinted up at me. 'And what's *your* name?' she asked.

It was the week before Labour Day and Shirley had invited me over to see her new kitten. I was a sucker for kittens, but I'd said yes mostly because I hoped Lester would be there. He wasn't.

The kitten was in a basket in the kitchen.

'Here,' Shirley said, picking it up and handing it to me. It was soft and white and the veined pink of its pointy ears showed through its fur.

'Hey, kitty kitty,' I said. 'What's your name?'

'I didn't give it a name yet,' Shirley said.

'Oh – well is it a girl cat?'

'I don't know,' she said.

The kitten opened its mouth wide, mewed once, and kneaded its paws against my chest. It had tiny vampire teeth. I asked Shirley how long she'd had it and she said, 'Since Wednesday. Mr Bemrose gave it to me.'

'Who?'

'Mr Bemrose. The math teacher.' She looked so saggy-eyed and tired I thought she might fall asleep at any moment. 'His cat had kittens.'

'So how come he gave *you* one?'

Shirley shrugged. 'He likes me. He gives me extra lessons.'

'Now? In summer?'

She nodded.

'Are you ever lucky,' I told her. 'It's the cutest thing.'

'I know.'

'Maybe you should call it Mr Bemrose. Or just plain Bemrose – in case it's a girl.'

Shirley stared at me blankly for a moment. 'No,' she said, frowning a little and blinking as if she were batting her eyes against fine drizzle. After a while she said, 'Mr Bemrose has got one leg shorter than the other. He wears special shoes.'

I stroked the kitten a little longer, then gave it back to Shirley. She put it in its basket and rubbed the top of its head. When she stood up, she said, 'Sometimes I get scared I'll squash it. I hug it and I just want to squeeze so hard I can feel it all the way through my teeth.'

Mrs Minty looked up from her magazine as I was leaving. Her eyebrows didn't match her hair. They were plucked into perfect black arches. 'You leaving already? Aren't you staying for dinner?'

'No, thank you,' I said. 'I have to go home.'

'My mother says come for dinner,' Shirley said one evening a couple of weeks later. She had a habit of starting right into a conversation without saying hello first. My father was working late at the store that night, so I agreed to go.

Shirley had done something to her hair. It was bright red. I told her I liked it and she looked pleased. 'It's a rinse,' she said, patting her hair, and then she said, 'I can do yours if you like.'

'That's okay,' I said.

Mrs Minty had to leave for the hospital before we ate. She came downstairs in her white lace-up shoes and starched nurse's uniform, smelling of stale smoke and hairspray. 'There's shepherd's pie in the oven. And there's canned peaches for dessert,' she told Shirley, and jabbed a thumb towards the living room, where Mr Minty was dozing on the couch. 'Wake him when you're ready.' Mrs Minty lit a cigarette and winked at me. Her eyes were the same green as Lester's. 'Dead to the world. Honestly, you could stick a firecracker under that man's butt, pardon my French, and you'd be lucky if he twitched. Shirley, give your little friend here some leftovers to take home to her father. I put the tinfoil on the counter to remind you. I don't know where the hell your brother's got to. Lester!' she hollered.

It took Shirley a while to wake Mr Minty. He seemed almost comatose. Finally he gave a sharp snore, shook his head and said, 'Wha?' By the time he got to the table, Lester, Shirley and I were already eating. He propped himself up on his elbows, yawned, squeezed his eyes shut a couple of times, looked at me and grunted. 'How you doing?' Then he said to Shirley, 'Your mother gone already? Whoa – what the hell happened to your hair?' When she handed him a plate of food, he perked up. He smothered it with ketchup, wolfed it down and helped himself to seconds. 'So,' he said to me in the middle of a mouthful. 'You the new kid?'

I told him I was. After a few more mouthfuls he said, 'You like it?'

I wasn't sure if he meant school or the neighbourhood or maybe the shepherd's pie, so I said, 'Yeah, I guess.'

He nodded. 'That's good.'

Nobody said much of anything for the rest of the meal. Mr Minty pushed his chair away from the table and got up while we were still eating. 'There's dessert,' Shirley said.

'What is it?'

'Canned peaches.'

'Again? I'll pass. Excuse me, ladies.' He gave Lester a friendly cuff on the back of the head and went back to the living room to watch TV.

Lester left soon after. 'You don't want dessert?' I asked him.

He snorted. On his way out he ignored Shirley, but he said, 'See you,' to me.

'Lester likes you,' Shirley said. 'I can tell.'

51

I helped her with the dishes. The kitten was asleep in the kitchen. It had grown since I last saw it, but she still hadn't given it a name.

Mr Bemrose used to limp slowly up and down the aisles, smoothing down his blow-dried hair, and if you were struggling with a math problem he'd drape his arm around your back, reach across your shoulder for your pen and scribble the solution in your book while he breathed warm mint and aftershave down your neck and murmured explanations in a voice smooth and thick as custard.

Once track season was underway, he'd call me up to the blackboard with a smirk on his face, hand me a piece of chalk and say, 'Let's see if our future Olympian can solve for x.'

While Mr Bemrose wrote equations on the board, Lester liked to lean into the aisle and flick rubber bands at his back. Mr Bemrose pretended he didn't notice, but his ears and neck would redden. 'Let's see if our future Olympian can zap Mr Bumroll's fat ass,' Lester whispered, passing me a couple of rubber bands. 'You get two shots. I'll give you five bucks if you hit his bald spot.'

'Sshh,' I hissed, trying to keep from giggling.

'Chickenshit,' Lester said.

Shirley Minty flat-out loved her brother Lester, even though he regularly arranged for boys to have sex with her after school. 'Um, do you know where Lester is? Have you seen my...?' she'd ask, her voice trailing off mid-sentence as she caught sight of him and spun off in his direction like a homing pigeon. She gazed rapturously at him in class, laughed at his lame jokes, took the rap for him when he was late, bought him cigarettes and candy bars. Lester seemed unimpressed. He'd stroke the little thread of pimples that dotted his jaw and say things like, 'You talking to me or chewing a brick?' Sometimes he cheerfully bopped her over the head with a ruler, or jabbed her arm, or squeezed her breasts, but mostly he ignored her.

On afternoons when the weather was okay, Lester and Shirley and an assortment of neighbourhood boys would go down into the ravine behind the junior high. I'd see them glance furtively about as they made their way down there in restless whispering clumps while I ran around the track, and I'd still be running when they came up again, slowly, in twos or threes, kicking dirt and grinning slyly as they took quick draws from cigarettes passed between them in cupped palms. I practised my start, crouching down and hurtling forward over and over while they sauntered across the lanes of the track. I sprinted hundred-metre dashes, arms pumping, legs and lungs burning, blood thrumming behind my eyes. Once, when I'd bent down to retie the laces of my spikes, Lester looked over at me and said something to whoever was beside him. They laughed out loud and I blushed so hard it made me dizzy. Lester winked at me, reached for the cigarette he'd tucked behind his ear, lit it, blew a few smoke rings and smiled his crocodile smile. Sometimes I saw him count the afternoon's takings as he walked, flipping through dollar bills like cards. Shirley straggled along, brushing bits of dead leaves and twigs from her hair, slapping mud and slugs from her knees and the backs of her legs. She'd give me a little wave, a baffled look on her face, and I'd keep on running until I thought my chest would burst.

Wendy Robinson was the most popular girl in seventh grade. 'Why do you hang around with Shirley Minty?' she asked me one morning during recess, her top lip curling scornfully as she spoke.

'I don't,' I replied.

'Yes, you do.' She tossed her blond hair back, thrust out her chest and sneered, hands on her hips.

'No, I don't. She lives on my street, that's all.'

Wendy shuddered. 'She's such a retard.'

'She's a slut,' Jill Podorowski added.

'A total slut,' Wendy agreed.

'I bet she does it with Mr Bemrose,' Trisha Speed said, and giggled.

'Eewww!' Jill's face twisted in disgust. She cupped her hand over her mouth.

Trisha fake-limped, patted her hair, draped herself over Wendy and sniffed her neck. Everyone doubled over laughing.

There were always rumours about Shirley. Whenever she missed a class, girls whispered that she had gotten pregnant, or been sent away to a convent, or caught the clap. They never said anything to her face, though. They kept away, as if they were scared sex could be catchy.

With Lester it was a different story. 'Hi, Lester,' Wendy Robinson chirped, smiling coyly as he went by. 'Hi, Lester,' the rest of them chorused.

By early spring, Wendy's crowd had started hanging out with Lester and his friends. They leaned against the hoods of cars and smoked. Wendy often showed up late after lunch, snapping her gum and rolling her eyes if Mr Bemrose said anything to her.

That spring, on days when there was no softball game or practice, I usually stayed after school and trained at the track on my own. One afternoon near the end of May, Mr Bemrose limped over while I was running. Shirley was heading off to the ravine with Lester and a group of boys, and Mr Bemrose cupped his hands over his mouth and shouted, 'Shirley!' but they were far away and none of them heard him. He stared after them until they disappeared down the slope. After a few moments he called out to me, 'Broken any records today?' He watched me circle the track, glancing towards the ravine from time to time, then he slowly limped away.

By the time Shirley walked back across the field, I was unlacing my spikes. Big black clouds were moving quickly overhead. Shirley came up to me and pointed at the sky. 'It's going to pour,' she said.

'I know,' I replied. 'I'm going home.'

Lester had gone on ahead with a few boys. 'They're going to hang out at Wendy's house,' Shirley said, and looked at me in a searching, mournful way.

I didn't say anything for a while. It had started to thunder, so we walked faster. When we were halfway home, I told her about Mr

Bemrose. 'He was calling you,' I said. 'He saw you go down there.'

'Oh,' she said. She didn't seem at all worried. 'I was supposed to have an extra lesson.'

'Did you forget?' I asked.

She said, 'No. I didn't feel like it.'

'Won't you get in trouble?'

She shrugged and shook her head.

Mrs Minty was waiting outside their house in her silver bikini, even though heavy raindrops had started to fall. She completely ignored me. Her hands were on her hips and her eyes were murderous. 'Where the hell have you been?' she asked Shirley.

'At extra math.'

'Don't you lie to me,' Mrs Minty yelled. 'Mr Bemrose called. I know what you've been up to. Where's that brother of yours?'

Shirley just stood there blinking, her wet mouth open.

We had math after recess the following day. Five minutes after class started, the secretary's voice came over the intercom, asking Mr Bemrose to please come down to the office. 'Page 136,' he said on his way out. 'Start working on examples 4 through 9. And keep it quiet.'

The minute he left, the noise began. Kids got up, threw things at one another, hooted and jeered. I glanced over at Shirley, who was staring morosely out the window. She'd looked miserable all morning. Trisha Speed went to the blackboard, grabbed a piece of yellow chalk and wrote, MR BEMROSE IS A PERV. Lester raised his eyebrows and in a prissy falsetto said, 'Ooh! Mr Bemrose is a perv, how shocking.'

'Watch out, guys,' someone called from the door. 'Here he comes!'

We were all back in our seats with textbooks open and pens in our hands when Mr Bemrose opened the door. A few kids had started to giggle, and soon there were titters all around the classroom. Mr Bemrose frowned and turned to look at the blackboard. 'All right,' he said, his face scarlet. 'Who wrote that?' Then he zeroed in on

Lester, who was leaning back in his chair with legs outstretched and arms folded across his chest, grinning. 'Wipe that stupid grin off your face,' Mr Bemrose snarled, 'or I'll wipe it off for you.'

Lester rocked upright in his chair and nodded slowly, pulling the corners of his mouth down, his green eyes narrowed and unblinking. Mr Bemrose limped over to him, glared at him for a moment, then smacked him hard across the face.

'Holy shit,' someone breathed. One of the girls whispered, 'Oh boy, Lester's gonna kill him.' But Lester just flinched and froze. Large finger-shaped welts sprang up on his cheeks and his eyes filled with tears. And then Shirley bolted from the classroom, knocking over a chair on her way.

Shirley was out of sight by the time Mr Bemrose motioned me outside. 'Go get her,' he said, pointing across the parking lot.

I sprinted leisurely, my feet springing from the tarmac, every stride jolting through my jaw. When I reached the sidewalk I saw Shirley running, her arms and legs flailing as she headed for the park at the end of the street. I gained on her easily, flying with the rush of adrenalin, my breath hard and steady.

I was about fifteen feet away and closing in fast when she turned her head briefly, her soft features jiggling as she ran, and our eyes locked for an instant. She looked shattered. 'Shirley,' I said. She spun around and kept going.

We were almost at the end of the park by the time I got close enough to touch her. My fingers grazed her wrist but she veered to the left, suddenly darting into the road.

There was a screech of brakes and Shirley's arms were reaching out, loose and slow, to stop the car, and the awful thud. And then there were people all around and finally Lester, pushing up alongside me, his face terrible.

Shirley was lucky. The car was travelling slowly and it turned out she'd only broken a leg, but she never came back to school that year, and sometime during the summer the Mintys moved away. Mr

Bemrose left immediately after the accident and we had a supply math teacher for the remainder of the semester.

There was a dance in the gym at the end of that school year. Lester asked if I wanted to dance, and after a few slow dances we went outside and walked down into the ravine. We sat on a fallen log, the dank night smell of early summer all around us and last winter's rotten leaves still on the ground. He had his arm around me and when we kissed he pushed his warm tongue into my mouth. Afterwards we walked hand in hand across the field, not saying a word, our fingers clamped tight together.

Years later I would still awaken to the look on Shirley's face before she dashed into the road. There was that sound, and her limp body lifting over the curved hood of the car. I'd lie tightly curled in the dark, thinking about how the two of us ran.

I often went down to the track on my own that summer. I would try to shut my mind down, concentrating only on the thud of my spikes on the ground and the painful rhythm of breath. Occasionally on weekends my father would come and watch me, and he'd sit in the bleachers with a stopwatch, timing my sprints. Sometimes I'd imagine the bleachers filled with spectators, everyone cheering as I tore around the track like a gale. And then there would be my mother, gliding towards me, her pale hands waving like someone drowning, my mother small in the distance then coming closer, the beautiful way she moved, from someplace far away.

MOST WANTED

Maddox didn't bother trying to stop his wife when she left him three months ago. He figured only a lunatic would imagine he could compete with Jesus.

'That's it? You're not even gonna try and make me stay?' Francie asked after he'd carried some of her stuff out to a van driven by a pale, plump, youngish woman named Hannah, one of the Born-Agains from the commune Francie moved to. Francie didn't take much with her – most things she'd boxed and tagged for charity.

Maddox shrugged. 'Waste of time.'

Hannah was standing tactfully off to the side with a smile on her blanched face, apparently transfixed by a squirrel's enthusiastic trapeze act. Her hands were clasped behind her back and every so often she'd rise up on tiptoes. She was humming something, her whole demeanour radiating righteousness, and Maddox half-expected her to burst into sudden full-throated song – Julie Andrews maybe, or a rollicking gospel number. Or else to levitate, her holy doughboy body hovering miraculously a few feet off the ground. He felt a dangerous hostility towards her.

Francie searched his face with her moist martyr-eyes. 'You could've at least *tried*,' she said.

Hannah's farewell handshake was about as limp and clammy as seaweed. Francie hugged him hard and promised to pray for him.

'Go ahead,' Maddox said, 'if it makes you feel good.' He opened the passenger door for her and gave the side of the van, which sported a predictable array of banal religious slogans, a couple of good-natured thumps as it pulled away. Much as one might slap the rump of a horse or a cow, he thought, or Hannah's ample ass. He waved them out of sight, aware as he did so that he was displaying admirable maturity and restraint through all this – hell, *grace* even – then he went inside, swallowed a Percodan (left over from Francie's gum surgery), lay down on the bed with his boots on and stared up at the ceiling for an hour or so. When he got up, he wandered into the kitchen, grabbed a beer and started flinging steak knives at the cross-stitched sampler Francie had embroidered and hung on the wall between the fridge and the stove. 'In the House of the Righteous Is Much Treasure,' the sampler proclaimed. There was another sampler in the bedroom, nailed slap-bang over the marital bed. 'Draw Nigh to God and He Will Draw Nigh to You,' that one said, which Maddox found at least as effective as a cold shower.

The phone rang. It was Francie. He could tell she'd been crying. 'What are you doing?' she asked.

'Fucking up the wall,' he answered, squinting at the gouged drywall where a knife had struck.

'I worry about you,' she told him.

He knew this would be a good moment to say, 'I miss you already. Please come home,' or something to that effect. Time to lay on the tenderness – she was already weepy; he was halfway there.

'The fuck you do,' is what Maddox said, hanging up the phone and aiming another steak knife at the sampler. From now on he'd keep score – twenty points for each embroidered letter.

Sure Signs of a Meltdown:
1. Using sampler as a dartboard.

In the three months since then, Maddox has gained thirteen pounds. He's also got himself a dog and a new Fender Stratocaster. He's making a mental list at the moment, Gained versus Lost (in between channel surfing and scarfing down nachos, the dog snoozing and drooling beside him on the couch). Thus far all he's come up with for Lost is Francie's awesome hash brownies. Double chocolate chip, moist and chewy, although he can't remember when last she baked them. Maddox has lately developed the habit of near-compulsive list-making – Twenty All-Time Favourite Movies; Best Blues Albums; Top Ten Reasons Not to Move to Budapest; Foods to Request on Death Row (the brownies top that list too); Five Most Wanted (he's already got the guitar and the dog, but still covets the BMW GS 1150 Adventure motorbike, a fifty-inch plasma TV and

Halle Berry). He adds sex to Lost, then changes his mind. He needs to join a gym.

Maddox finds Francie's evangelical zeal downright obnoxious. Fact is, she became a major drag after her lightning-bolt conversion. She used to be fun, she'd been wild, she was an ex-*groupie* for Chrissakes (one or two of INXS, most of Guns N' Roses and a handful of roadies, as far as he knows) and then all of a sudden there she was organizing revival meetings and singing hymns on street corners while handing out pamphlets urging redemption. She approached religion with the same enthusiasm she'd previously directed to aromatherapy and Tantric sex, developing self-righteousness and a ridiculously serene *glow*. Night after night he'd find her sitting there glowing away piously with the New Testament open on her lap as gospel-era Dylan or the Mighty Clouds of Joy trumpeted through the house.

And yet Maddox can't shake the belief that he's largely responsible for her transformation. Unintentionally so, but responsible nevertheless.

What happened was this: two years ago he and Francie were living in a soon-to-be-condemned loft on the top floor of a disused zipper factory. A pizza delivery guy rang the doorbell one evening while Maddox was playing his electric guitar. The building was ancient, the wiring faulty, and when Maddox stopped strumming long enough to turn the metal doorknob with his right hand (his fretting hand still holding a chord on the neck of the guitar), he became part of the circuit and fried himself. Francie told him later that the pizza delivery guy was crawling around the floor frantically, using the broom to tug at every cord in sight. She straddled Maddox's waist, pounded his chest with her small fists and screamed at him. That's when the praying started. Until the paramedics arrived, she gave Maddox mouth-to-mouth, and each time she lifted her head to take another breath she somehow managed to keep on screaming at him and pleading and bargaining with God. She was still praying hours later while he lay recuperating in a hospital bed. Whenever Maddox opened his eyes Francie was at his side, eyes squeezed shut and lips barely moving as she whispered her soft prayers. Her childlike hand fluttered over his bandage, coming to rest on it briefly from time to time, light as a hummingbird.

'Give it a rest,' he mumbled a couple of times, but if she heard she took no notice.

Maddox came away from this close call with the strings of a Stratocaster forever branded in deep grooves across the fingers of his left hand, and Francie came away with Religion.

Comparisons to Jesus:
1. I too am no slouch as a carpenter.
2. I once had a beard (okay, a goatee. For six weeks max. But still).
3. Soulful eyes.

The dog, Duane, just about breaks Maddox's heart. He's a three-legged mutt Maddox rescued from the pound shortly after Francie's departure. Duane lost his left foreleg in an incident of abuse too terrible to contemplate – something involving an apartment building's garbage chute – and he has at least one metal pin in his hip and/or spine. The dog-adoption lady at the pound told Maddox the damage wasn't only physical. 'The poor thing still gets depressed. Bless him,' she sighed, and Maddox had to suppress an intense urge to wrap his arms around this matronly woman who blessed poor mutts like Duane, even though her mutt-blessing might indicate religious tendencies that would normally piss him off. But it isn't Duane's occasional bouts of depression that bother Maddox (episodes in which the dog just sits there, bracing himself on his remaining foreleg and staring morosely at the ground for unbelievably long periods) so much as the flip side – the dog's irrational *optimism* in the face of such a raw deal. It's the way he hobbles eagerly after squirrels or Frisbees or non-disabled dogs in the park, all waggling excitement to begin with until he finally stops and quivers, no doubt realizing there's no way he'll ever be coordinated or fast enough to get by in this world, but thumping his stoic tail nevertheless and grinning pathetically as if to console Maddox; or the way he loses his balance from time to time and topples over, righting himself with a sneeze and a sheepish tilt of the head. Even thinking about these things is enough to make Maddox want to weep.

But Maddox is not above using the sorry creature as a magnet for tenderhearted women. They look stricken when they first see Duane, then they crouch and slap their knees, cooing, 'Aw! Come over here,' and Maddox gives them small sad smiles and thinks, *Bingo!*

His latest job – built-in entertainment and shelving units of cherry and curly maple, which he started to make a couple of days ago for a droopy little fashionista whose name escapes him – came from just such an encounter. The fashionista (Paula? Sheila? Lauren?) wore a miniskirt and stiletto-heeled knee-high boots for a walk in the park with her skittish borzoi. 'Maddox?' she'd murmured while scratching poor Duane's ears with her tastefully manicured fingernails. She was gazing at Maddox with such fierce sincerity she looked almost cross-eyed. 'Is that your first name?' The fashionista, who's an entertainment lawyer, is slouch-shouldered with seal-sleek hair and a narrow face. She has the weird pointed intensity of a long-necked exotic bird – an ibis or emu, or maybe an ostrich. 'I'm a total design maniac. Honestly, I *worship* great design,' she announced when she hired him, and Maddox finds it amusing that her hugely expensive new midtown condo is actually an eighth of a renovated church. Standing in the cathedral-ceilinged living room, with mid-afternoon light flashing through the clerestory windows, Maddox asked what sort of look she was after for the wall units. Photographs of his work were spread across the coffee table, alongside lacquered bowls filled with wasabi rice crackers and piri-piri root chips and organic tapenade. Paula/Sheila/Lauren was wearing low-slung jeans and a back-baring suede halter-top that Maddox found mildly arousing. 'Something high end,' she replied, frowning as she gazed at the empty wall. 'Different, but classy.' She looked at Maddox and nodded earnestly. 'I've got a lot of faith in you. Really. Just go ahead and knock me out with the design.' Her thin arms were held at her sides like snapped wings. *Peck, peck*, he thought, and nodded back.

As if Maddox's life weren't enough for her, Francie became hell-bent on saving his soul as well. 'Listen. Whatever gets you through the night, I don't care. Just count me out,' he told her, but it did no good.

Shortly before she left, she presented him with a list of conditions. On top of the page was written *Wish List*, and underneath that Francie had listed about a dozen items in her loopy script.

'What the hell is this?'

'My wish list,' she replied quietly, nodding for emphasis. 'Things I want you to do. To see if we can put us back together again.'

It was a pitiful list. As Maddox recalls, it went something like this:

1. Come to church, at least on Sundays.
2. Attend revival meetings, once a month minimum.
3. Stop getting wasted.
4. Cut the blasphemy.
5. Quit belittling me about my faith,

and so on. There was also

11. Chew properly,

which had nothing to do with her religious fervour – she just hated the way he ate.

'Jesus. Don't you think this is a bit much?' Maddox waved the piece of paper in front of Francie's nose. 'I mean, how about a little give and take here, a little tit for tat? What do you say we trade?'

Her face tightened. 'Trade?'

'Yeah. Let's do a little exchange. Like, say, a revival meeting for a couple of blowjobs. Or three. Hell, it's worth at *least* three.'

Francie just sat there staring at the floor and looking as if she might cry. Maddox reached for her fist but she pulled it away. 'Christ,' he said, not unkindly. 'What the hell has happened to you?'

Finally she looked up at him and in a tired voice said, 'Just so you know. This stuff is not negotiable.'

The fashionista, who named her borzoi Manolo, after the shoe designer, drew a blank on Duane. 'Who?' she asked in her sharp, birdlike way, then shrugged dismissively when Maddox explained. 'I'm not really big on guitarists,' she told him.

Francie, on the other hand, never missed a beat. Her taste in music might have spiralled embarrassingly south lately (Mercy Me? Amy Grant, for Chrissakes?) but when Maddox told her about his new three-legged pal she said, 'Duane, huh. So you named your dog after an Allman brother?'

This was during one of their late-night phone calls. At first it was always Francie who did the calling. 'Hey, Francie!' Maddox would say. 'How's it going in zombie land?' She whispered so she wouldn't wake the other Born-Agains. 'You could call me too sometimes, you know. It wouldn't kill you.'

Maddox began calling every now and then when he couldn't find things – documents, box-cutters, spare chequebooks. The first time he called he was put on hold for about five minutes. Instead of Muzak, he had to listen to a recording of a jarringly chirpy woman's voice: 'These beautiful pewter crown-of-thorns lapel pins and pendants are a one-time offer. The pendants are on an attractive leather thong and both pieces come with a handy satin drawstring pouch for storage. They're available for purchase at the church office for twenty-nine ninety-nine each, or from our website at soulredemption.com. New witness kits are also now available at the office, and Trucker Dan is presently transporting these kits to our brethren across the country. Let us all give thanks and pray for their safe delivery, and for a blessed journey for Trucker Dan. The annual bake sale and bazaar takes place on the fifteenth ...'

'Hello?' Francie sounded worried.

'Hi. So did you get your crown-of-thorns necklace yet?'

'My what?'

'Never mind. Where's the plant spray? There's an infestation here.'

'Should be in the laundry cupboard. Behind the shoe polish. An infestation?'

'Yep. A nasty one. Aphids.'

'Uh-oh. You're not going to kill them, are you?'

He'd forgotten about Thou Shalt Not Kill, Not Even Aphids. 'Hell no, I'm just planning to stun them with a light mist of insecticide.'

There was silence on the other end of the line.

'Don't worry, I'll bless them first. Let them say their prayers and save their little souls before they buy the farm. They'll all go straight to aphid heaven, I promise. Unless I can find some ants real quick.'

'You lost me.'

'They herd them.'

'What are you talking about?'

'Ants. They love aphids. Aphids are ant cows.'

'You're making this up.'

'No, I'm not. Aphids give off some kind of secretion the ants go crazy for. They corral them, take them back to the ant heap and milk them. I'm not kidding. They stroke them and sweet-talk them and the aphids give them what they want. It's a beautiful thing.'

'I don't know, Maddox. Where do you *get* this stuff?'

'Hey, listen to this,' he said casually, as if he'd just thought of it, reaching for his acoustic guitar and placing the phone in front of him so she could hear him play something new.

Aside from Francie's irritating habit of quoting from the Scriptures, Maddox has come to realize he actually looks forward to her calls. He is comforted by the easy intimacy they've settled into on the phone, and besides, her inane jabber about abounding love and light and miracles works better than any sleeping pill. He listens to her go on and on and feels the tightness in his jaw dissolve with the slow rise and fall of her voice.

'Pastor Jenkins went on a rampage this morning,' she'll whisper as she brings him up to speed on commune gossip and fills him in on the day-to-day stuff – the veggie prep and bookkeeping and admin for which they pay her diddly squat ('Yeah, but there's really nothing I need,' Francie, who went and shut down her aromatherapy practice when she moved out, insists); the hours of Bible study; the sing-alongs and suppers and the histrionics of Pastor Jenkins, who scares his flock witless with his palsied rants about a Hell so dark you couldn't see your own hand in front of your face, so hot your flayed flesh would sizzle and curl from your blistered bones in festering strips, whereupon the faithful moan and sob and shout their Glad Amens and Hallelujahs and Praise the Lords and the newly saved flop down wailing and babbling, their dripping noses pressed to the carpet.

'Sounds pretty dramatic.'

'Oh, you have *no* idea.'

One evening she was giving him the lowdown on her evangelical excursions with the rest of the door-to-door devout. 'Witnessing and Inviting,' she called it, telling him they fan out and work a neighbourhood in pairs. Her Witnessing and Inviting partner is the pale and ample-assed Hannah.

He said, 'God salesmen, that's what you are.'

Her enthusiastic response surprised him: 'That's it!'

'Remember Balsam Avenue?' he said. 'Those Jehovah's Witnesses?'

A couple of stiff-hipped Watchtower-proffering women had shown up one too many Saturday mornings – ridiculously early, as always – at the place they were renting five or six years ago. This time he and Francie were ready for them. They waited until the unsuspecting pair came trundling up the front walk, then dropped their jeans and mooned the Witnesses, yelling, 'Hey, ladies, witness *this!*' as they shoved their bare asses up against the screen door. They'd whooped and gasped with laughter while the women retreated in hasty slack-jawed horror, cheeks flapping, elbows and copies of the Watchtower flying every which way.

'Bet they never knew they could run so fast.'

'Yeah, well,' she said after a long pause. 'There's a whole lot of things I'm not exactly proud of.'

'I don't know, Francie. Why couldn't you just become a Unitarian, or a run-of-the mill Methodist or something? Why does everything have to be so goddamn *extreme?*'

What I really miss about Francie:

1. That incredible thing she used to do with her tongue.
2. How she twitches in her sleep like a kid.
3. The way she plays with her hair while she reads, even the Bible.
4. All those years she'd listen to 'Stairway to Heaven' first thing in the morning.

Lately Maddox has been telling Francie about the fashionista, hoping to make her jealous.

'You would not believe this woman's condo,' he said.

'"Unless the Lord builds the house, they labour in vain who build it,"' was her smug response.

He has also mentioned Francie to the fashionista. Yesterday morning, over a mochaccino in her new state-of-the-art kitchen, it slipped out before he could stop himself. 'My wife left me. Actually, not that long ago,' he said, raising his eyebrows and biting the corner of his lower lip.

'God. That's terrible.'

'Yep. Three months ago. She left me for Jesus, you believe that?' He gave a little snorting laugh. 'I mean, talk about being out of my league.'

'Boy,' she said slowly, as if giving this information serious thought.

There was no stopping him once he got started. He held up his scarred fingers. 'You see these?'

'Oh wow.' She squinted at the skin grafts and sucked in air with what appeared to be genuine sympathy, but since her default expression was genuine sympathy he couldn't be certain.

He told her about his near-electrocution, about Francie's shocking transformation, about the subsequent bitter wrangling for his soul. He even told her about Francie's hash brownies.

'Now there I can help you,' the fashionista said. 'There's a guy who makes these unbelievable biscotti. I'm talking *incredible*. Like, all you need is a quarter – a whole one would do you in.' She patted his damaged hand. 'Tell you what. If you come to my party tonight,

I'll order some, just for you.' Maddox started to make an excuse, but she said, 'Come on, it's my birthday.'

She was flirting with him, he realized, in her weird birdlike way. 'Really? Happy birthday,' he drawled, grinning at her.

'Oh, thank you,' she said coyly, then snared him with her ultra-sincere gaze. 'It's no big deal, but you know, there's just so much horrible stuff going on in the world. We have to celebrate every chance we get. No really, I truly believe that. This place isn't finished yet but what the heck. It'll be very low key, just some good friends. And hey, it's Friday night. Please come.'

He showed up late, bearing a bromeliad, which had seemed perfect for her with its single bizarre pink flower spiking from an improbably thin stem.

'Aw. That is so *sweet*,' she gushed, air-pecking both his cheeks and placing the plant on the hallstand with her other gifts. Apparently all except his were lavishly wrapped. 'Come get a drink and meet everyone. Everyone, this is Maddox. He makes *great* furniture.' She leaned in close and whispered conspiratorially, 'Ta da! See? Biscotti.' She pointed to a plate on a side table. 'I had to cut them up so people don't get totally wasted. Butchered them a bit but hey, they taste the same. They take a while to kick in but they're *so good*. Ooh, Maddox, here, meet Bill, my designer. He's brilliant. You both are, you're both brilliant. You guys should talk.'

Maddox refrained from sharing his theory on interior designers, which is that they are entirely superfluous (his logic being as follows: your space should reflect your own personality, therefore unless you're willing to totally negate yourself and live inside someone else's personality, you should not hire one, ever). 'How's it going,' he nodded.

Bill looked him up and down and gave a strained smile. 'Not bad. So you make furniture? You have to show me your portfolio,' he said unconvincingly.

'You'll absolutely love his stuff. You two talk. I'll be right back,' the fashionista said, and she drifted off to another pair of guests.

Bill said, 'God, I love her. She's something, isn't she?'

'That she is.' After a minute or two Maddox said, 'Excuse me. I need a drink.' He poured himself a double single malt and ate a couple of pieces of biscotti, which tasted pretty good, although nowhere near as good as Francie's brownies, and then he sampled some of the various mysterious-looking snacks. The room was full of botoxed strangers – media people and producers and lawyers and actors – with a couple of scowling artists thrown in for texture. He attempted to join in a few conversations but nobody seemed particularly interested in him. The fashionista was flitting from group to group, chirping and giggling in a droopy, manic way. The biscotti hadn't even taken the edge off, so he had some more. In desperation he tried to latch onto Bill, the designer, who was talking to a couple of gorgeous women. 'Hey,' Maddox said, and they flashed bored smiles at him. All three of them, Maddox noticed, had luscious lips – swollen Angelina Jolie lips, with a life of their own. He became conscious of his own mouth hanging open, gaping in fascination at Collagen Central.

'Oh hi,' Bill said. 'Sorry, I forgot your name.'

'Maddox.'

'Maddox, right. So anyway,' he said, turning back to the women, 'he's delicious, but kinda shy. I mean, he's from *Saskatchewan*. So I'm going to have to be Farm Boy Bill. Forget Rock 'n' Roll Bill, my fucked-up bellbottoms? Tight butt? Rock 'n' Roll Bill does not *exist* for this guy. But I can do it. It's all there in my closet. Farm Boy Bill is in my closet. Got the shirt, got the pants, got the hat.' He put his hands on his hips and shimmied. 'Girl, I can *do* this.'

Maddox reflected that this was definitely one personality you didn't want to be living in. He drifted back to the biscotti and the mysterious-looking snacks, which tasted increasingly good. A woman standing nearby was giving him bemused sidelong glances and he realized he was eating compulsively. He suddenly felt very stoned, but it didn't make anything any easier. It was an intense whole-body kind of stoned, and he could barely move. All he could think about was how much he wanted to lie down, and maybe call Francie if it wasn't too late.

'Already?' the fashionista wailed when he told her he was leaving.

He mumbled something about needing to get back to Duane. 'I think he's sick. He was shivering when I left,' he lied. His jaw was so relaxed that he found it difficult to speak.

'Aw. The poor thing.' The fashionista's face crumpled with concern. 'Oh wait, before you go.' She scooped the rest of the biscotti into a Ziploc and handed it to Maddox. 'Here, take these,' she said, folding her hand over his as he grasped the bag. She was gazing at him and for a moment Maddox thought of staying. He could lie down here for a while, on her bed, and wait to see how things would play out. She glanced at his damaged hand, then squinted up at him and cocked her head to the side. 'Something I've been meaning to ask you,' she said. 'Just a quick question.'

'Shoot.'

'Ah – I was just wondering. With that electric shock – how did it feel?'

Maddox gave a quick laugh and shook his head. 'In how many words?'

The fashionista released her grasp. 'Sorry. Stupid question.' She patted him gently on the back. 'Go,' she said. 'Take care of poor Duane.'

What I really miss about Francie:

5. She knows I'm feeling down when I play 'Hey Joe' over and over.

It was late and he was too wasted when he got home last night, so Maddox never did get to speak to Francie, even though she'd left him two messages. Her voice sounded small and needy the second time, saying, 'Me again. Just wanted to talk. Where are you?'

It's already Saturday evening and he still hasn't called back. He turns off the TV, picks off the stray bits of nachos that have landed on his T-shirt and pops them into his mouth, and reaches for the cordless phone. Duane stirs, looks up at him and sighs deeply. Maddox dials the number but nobody answers. Eventually he gets the commune's answering machine and hangs up without leaving a message.

He goes into the kitchen and opens the fridge. Not much in it except beer, milk, bread and salsa. Not much in the freezer either, other than the fashionista's Ziploc. He eats a couple of pieces of biscotti while he watches Duane come hobbling through the kitchen door. 'This is ridiculous, you know that?' Maddox says. 'We have to get you a prosthetic leg.' Duane thumps his tail expectantly against the linoleum. 'Sorry boy, there's fuck-all to eat here. Wanna go pick up a couple of burgers?'

He helps Duane onto the front passenger seat of the pickup and heads for the drive-thru. When their order is ready he pulls into a parking bay, unwraps Duane's burger (no mustard, no pickles) and lays it on the seat between them. The whole thing's gone in two seconds flat except for half the bun, and then Duane whines for more so Maddox tosses him a few fries. The dog inhales them and starts whining again, shuffling until he falls sideways against the backrest. 'Forget it,' Maddox says, turning away and looking out the side window while he eats. When he finishes he sits there and watches the traffic a while, then starts the engine, pulls up alongside a garbage receptacle, opens the window all the way and plays garbage-bin basketball with the balled-up wrappings and Duane's unfinished bun. 'You ready to go home?' he says to Duane, but when he's about to make the turn he changes his mind and heads in the opposite direction.

The commune is a sprawling place on the northeastern outskirts of the city. A big tattooed guy who looks like an ex-con is standing and smoking outside. He eyes Maddox and Duane as they approach and Maddox wonders if this is Trucker Dan.

'Hi,' Maddox says. He can hear people singing in the distance. 'Francie here?'

The guy nods, takes a final deep drag and flicks the cigarette away. 'I believe so.' He smiles down at Duane, jerks his head to indicate that Maddox should follow him and they go around the side of the house, slowly because of Duane, to the backyard. The Born-Agains are sitting around the campfire on lawn chairs or cross-legged on the grass. They're all glowing in the firelight and singing religious songs. Someone's playing bad acoustic guitar and the others shake tambourines or clap or do a little hand jive on the beat. When they notice the ex-con/Trucker Dan standing there with Maddox and Duane, the singing falters and peters out. Francie, who has her back to Maddox, turns, gives a little squeal and claps her hand over her mouth as she scrambles to her feet.

'Is something wrong?' she whispers when she reaches him.

Maddox is trembling. He shakes his head and she hugs him. Her long hair is tousled and her face and neck are soft and hot from the fire. 'I tried calling,' he says.

Francie takes his hand and squeezes. 'This is Maddox,' she announces to everyone, beaming. 'My husband.' They're all gazing at him with a sweet kind of wonder, as if he were a being who came from another world. 'And I guess you already met Pastor Jenkins,' she says happily, motioning to the ex-con/Trucker Dan.

Pastor Jenkins nods and smiles. 'Come and join us,' he says, pointing to the campfire.

'And Duane,' Francie says, bending forward to pat him.

'Ah, that's okay,' Maddox tells Pastor Jenkins. 'I came to talk to my wife.'

Francie keeps squeezing his hand and grinning as she leads him into the house.

'Do you call each other Brother and Sister?'

He feels her stiffen and withdraw. 'What?'

'You know, like Sister Francie? Brother Dan? Sister Hannah?'

'No. Why would we do that?'

'I don't know. Just wondering. Were you toasting marshmallows out there?'

She gives him a slow smile. 'Yes, as a matter of fact.'

Her room is small, with two sets of bunk beds facing one another. She sits on one of the lower bunks and pats the covers for him to sit beside her. 'This one's mine,' she says. 'I fell off the top

73

bunk my first night here. Now I get claustrophobic.' She massages Duane's back and he nuzzles closer.

'I got your messages. You sounded terrible.'

'Yeah? Sorry. I had a bad day. I'm okay. Some days I need to pray harder, that's all. I need to ask Jesus to come into my heart.'

Maddox leans back against the wall. Above them is a calendar filled with coloured stars, taped to the underside of the top bunk. 'What's with all the stars?'

She leans back beside him and rubs her index finger over a star. 'Impure thoughts,' she says. 'Every time we have them we're supposed to stick a star on that day. Victory is a day with no stars.'

'All your days have stars.'

'I know.'

He says, 'What kind of impure thoughts?'

Francie shrugs and looks away. 'I don't know. About you mostly, I guess.' When she turns back he sees she's been crying a little. Duane nudges his snout against her leg because she's stopped stroking him. 'He's a nice dog,' she says, wiping her eyes and patting him again. 'The thing is, I can't stop thinking about you. It's like I'm missing my front teeth or something.'

'So come home.'

'And then what?' After a while she says, 'There's marriage counselling, you know. At the church.'

'What, through prayer?' he says sharply. He looks up at the calendar stars. 'God. I wish we'd never ordered that fucking pizza. We should've gone out for Chinese.'

'No, don't say that.'

'Why? Because everything's part of the Lord's plan? Bullshit, Francie.'

Duane nudges her again, his tail wagging. 'Poor fella.' She plays with his ears for a few minutes then says, 'Weird how you and Duane have this affliction, you know? Both on the left side.'

'Affliction?' Maddox holds up his hand. 'You think this is an *affliction?* Christ, I'm not an amputee.'

'It was a message,' she explains patiently.

'What? For you? To repent? How come you always thought this was about you? Not once did you ask how it felt to be nearly electrocuted, you know that? Not once. As far as you're concerned it's always been about you.'

'You're wrong.' She shakes her head sadly. 'I always thought it was about *us*.'

'Anyway,' Maddox says. He sighs. 'It's getting late.'

Francie just sits there looking like she's going to cry again. Maddox puts his arm around her and holds her close. After a couple of minutes he says, 'You know where to find me.'

'Me too,' she says in a flat voice.

He hates leaving her like this, in this Spartan room with her stick-on stars and all the relentless praying and self-deprivation. He takes out his wallet, because he has no idea how else to change anything, and peels off four twenty-dollar bills. 'Here. Take this.'

Her face goes blank. 'Oh no. I don't want your money.'

'In case you need anything. Please.'

She gestures around the room. 'Honestly. There's nothing.'

He keeps holding out the money even though he realizes it's stupid. 'Come on, buy yourself something. I don't know, a necklace or something. Or give it to the church. I don't care.'

She refuses to take it, but when she walks out the room ahead of him, Maddox slips the money under her pillow.

When he gets home there's a voice-mail message from the fashionista: 'Maddox, hi, it's Laura. Just calling to see how Duane's doing and um, I'm really sorry you couldn't stay last night. Hope you're both okay. Talk to you soon.'

He starts to dial her number, then hangs up. He has no idea what to say. He supposes he could try explaining to her what it was like when that electric jolt charged through him; how the current had hooked him and he'd felt every jerking nerve and muscle contract hard around it until he spun off into a white fog. But that would be all.

After a while he gets up and plugs the Stratocaster into the amplifier. He ignores the phone when it rings. As he plays he thinks of Francie and how she is lost to him, and then the Born-Agains come to mind – the way they were earlier, all of them gleaming, their faces lit and floating like planets around the campfire. The phone rings again several times and the red message light flashes steady as a strobe but Maddox just closes his eyes and keeps on playing, well into the night.

THE BENDING MOMENTS OF BEAMS

The day we moved here, three years ago, Jake and Tasmin and I sat on boxes in the centre of this room and ate takeout Chinese. I looked around at the freshly painted walls, the polished hardwood floors, at our boxes and my drawing board and the fern I'd hung on the hook above the window. My heart knocked huge against my rib cage, throbbing with fear and exhilaration on its uncertain way to freedom and I thought: *It will hold, it is enough.*

It's eight-thirty at night and I'm at my drafting table, working on the design for the Haydens' renovation, listening to some old Dylan. 'Idiot wind,' he sings. Howard's coming over to pick up his stuff. I've piled it in the middle of the living room floor.

Tacked to a corner of my drawing board is the picture I tore from a magazine yesterday. It's a photograph of an open gold lipstick case with a lethal-looking knife blade where the lipstick should be. The caption reads, 'If Lips Could Kill'. I can't decide if it's a weapon, a work of art, a fashion accessory, or some sort of political statement. Imagine an attacker holding off while his victim prepares to reapply lipstick – *Just give me a moment to freshen up* – then she stabs him in the eye. Perhaps it could be used on the Other Woman: *Here, let me try this lipstick on you – such a unique red.*

I pour myself more of Howard's Glenfiddich and imagine drawing the cold steel tip of the lipstick-knife along the outline of my mouth. I picture Howard coming in and I'm grinning madly, blood spreading along my teeth and oozing down my chin. *One last kiss, for old time's sake*, I'll say, and run my tongue like a vamp along blood-darkened lips. Afterwards I'd have a scar like permanent lip liner, a thin weal that would stretch when I smile.

Wounds close, blood congeals, torn flesh fuses. Scars form like photographic images we retain as reminders of difficulties or triumphs. This patched tissue is resilient – my son Jake was delivered by

Caesarean section, and throughout my next pregnancy, with Tasmin, I watched my ballooning belly as the long thick welt that bisects it stretched impossibly taut and shiny. *It'll burst*, I worried, *it can't possibly hold*, but it did. Strong, but sensitive. When Lars – my ex-husband – or Howard or anyone else traced fingertips or tongues along the ridged length of the scar, I couldn't bear it.

It wasn't my affair with Lars's partner or his affair with the travel agent that caused our marriage to collapse. It wasn't the boredom, or the battles over bank loans or the children or who would mow the lawn. It's a slow accumulation until you push each other a little too far and one day you find yourself alone in the middle of an empty room, the fury of the final argument still reverberating.

With a building, you design according to the maximum anticipated loads; you create a careful balance of concrete, steel, glass and wood that barely trembles under the shifting weight of people, snow, wind and walls. You aim for equilibrium so that supports will neither hog nor sag under the action of loads and reactions. You use equations to calculate that beams are of sufficient size and strength to resist the forces that will act upon them. Before even one nail has been hammered in, you can determine the point at which the maximum bending moment occurs, the place where the beam will tend to sag, buckle, snap. Of course, there are miscalculations: department stores or parking garages crumple; wood heaves and splinters; metal groans and twists.

While the lecturer scribbled mathematical calculations on the blackboard during Theory of Structures classes, I'd think of swimming underwater as beams of sunlight slanted through the surface, or I'd imagine a lithe young gymnast teetering on a balance beam, dipping pointed toes as she pliéd, turning over in a slow cartwheel then bending backwards, pelvis thrust up, gripping the beam with hands and feet, holding perfectly still for a moment.

I lower the volume on the tape deck. Kitchen cabinets and drawers are being opened and slammed shut. Plates and cutlery clink on the counter.

'Tasmin,' I call. 'Tasmin? That you?'

She slouches in. 'What.'

She's carrying a bowl of Rocky Road ice cream. Tasmin is fifteen, long and lean.

'You okay?'

'Yeah. Why wouldn't I be?' Scowling. 'What did you call me for?'

'Just to see how you're doing.'

'Oh. So can I go now?'

I shrug. 'Sure.'

She slinks off, then a minute later swings back in. 'What's all that stuff doing in the middle of the floor?'

'It's Howard's. He's coming by to collect it.'

She stares at me, unblinking. 'You're really going through with this?'

She's barefoot, wearing low-slung baggy jeans and a cropped tank top. Her hair is twisted up off her long neck. Everything is smooth, unblemished, lucent. And she's pouting.

I first met Howard about a year ago. I'd invited my ex-shrink over for dinner because I was so excited to find out she was still alive – I'd heard she killed herself, then one evening, months later, I saw her standing in line outside a movie theatre.

She brought Howard along to dinner, introducing him as an old friend. He told me he worked as a sportscaster at an all-news radio station, and he looked me over in a way that made me want to shove out my arms and say, *Hey, back off*. He seemed pumped – talking loudly in a rapid-fire sportscaster's voice – and he sniffed a lot. I decided he could have a summer cold, or more likely he'd done a couple of lines of coke before dinner.

The evening was going badly. Claudia, my ex-shrink, had too much to drink. 'It seems the only aptitude you need to be a sportscaster,' she drawled, spearing a slice of grilled sweet potato with her fork, 'is the ability to think of a variety of words that mean win, or lose. Correct me if I'm wrong, Howard. But you guys say, The Braves *blanked* the Expos six three. The Indians *shut out* the Jays five nothing. The Rockets *trailed* the Vikings seventeen ten – '

'That'd be tough,' Howard said, grinning, 'since we're talking totally different sports here – '

'Whatever,' Claudia said. 'You know what I mean. You can't just say, Such-and-such-a-team won. It has to be they ran roughshod over. They humbled. They pummelled, they wasted, they downed. Or my favourite – they exed. Don't you love that one? Exed. She exed him.'

We had coffee and dessert out on the patio. There were thick low clouds, the air was terribly still, and I felt the start of a headache. Claudia's eyes drifted restlessly, and Howard's leg jiggled incessantly. He sniffed and frowned and chewed on his lower lip.

'So,' Claudia said to me, 'you're still making good, safe spaces for people to live in?'

I shrugged. Smiled. Wished they'd go home.

'The million-dollar question,' she continued, 'is how does one construct a good, safe *life?*'

'I guess that's your department,' I said.

'Well, you make plans, you factor in all the variables. You design everything perfectly, you've got it all figured out,' she opened her arms wide, then let them fall to her sides. 'And chances are, it's still going to fall apart.'

I nodded, and offered more coffee. The headache was getting worse.

'Forget perfection,' Howard said. 'The thing is to find someone who'll love you right. You have to walk around with your eyes wide open. Grab whatever happiness you can. Grit your teeth through the disappointments.'

He was looking at me – his eyes amused, the corners of his mouth twitching slightly – and I held my breath. The space between us became a physical thing, as if it could be touched, weighed, measured, and I suddenly knew I was going to sleep with him. The way you realize, with a thrilled shudder, that you are still capable of ruining your life.

'Hmmm,' Claudia said softly, watching us. 'The touching, heartbreaking ways we limp along. Wobbly, but brave.'

The next time Howard came to dinner was to meet Jake and Tasmin.

'They'll be difficult,' I'd warned.

'It's okay. I have nieces and nephews.'

Tasmin refused to get off the phone when Howard arrived. When she finally came to say hello, twenty minutes later, she barely looked at him, and mumbled or shrugged when he attempted conversation.

'She's angry,' I told him when she went off to make another phone call. 'She doesn't want anyone replacing Lars.'

'That's understandable,' Howard said.

I'd known him for two weeks. We could barely keep our hands off one another.

'Teenage girls are impossible,' I said. 'Their hormones are all over the map. Boys are easier to deal with. They shut themselves in their rooms and refuse to communicate, and they do stuff like break into warehouses, but they don't say terrible things to their mothers. Girls have no problem communicating. They over-communicate. They weep and wail, they tell you they love you, they scream that they wish you'd go away and die. It's like living with a human yo-yo.'

Jake came in as we were sitting down to eat. He had a part in a school play, and rehearsals ran late.

Tasmin turned up her nose at the gazpacho. 'What else is there?' she asked, and sighed when I told her. She whined that she was missing *90210*.

'It's reruns,' Jake said. 'You've probably seen this episode fifty times.'

'I don't see why I have to stay,' she said. 'I hate listening to people eat.'

Eventually I gave in. She took a tray of food and went off to watch TV. 'She has this phobia,' I explained to Howard. 'It drives her crazy when other people chew.'

'She's in serious need of therapy,' Jake said.

Jake decided Howard was okay. He had a cool job, and he promised Jake baseball tickets. They discussed movies and music and sports.

One down, I thought.

After dinner I apologized for Tasmin's behaviour.

'Don't worry,' Howard said. 'She'll come 'round.'

She did come around. Howard commiserated with her over homework. He laughed with her during *The Simpsons* and *Seinfeld* reruns. He praised her pottery masks and figurines, so she made him a salad bowl shaped like half a football.

By the time Howard moved in with us, six months later, he'd started teaching Jake to drive.

'No way I could do it,' I said. 'I'd need tranquillizers.'

'As soon as you turn sixteen, I'll teach you,' he promised Tasmin. She still refused to eat with us.

'Hey, Mom,' Jake says. 'What's up?'

'Not much. Just working on this renovation.'

'How come you put Howard's stuff in the middle of the floor?'

'He's stopping by tonight to pick it up. You feel okay about all this, Jake?'

'About Howard leaving?' His hands are shoved into his pockets. He shifts his weight from foot to foot. 'Yeah. He's a shithead.'

Last Saturday I'd arranged to meet some clients at their country retreat a hundred kilometres away to discuss renovating the place. Howard was out running errands when I left.

I'd been driving for about twenty minutes when my cell phone rang. The clients had to cancel the meeting – their car broke down.

Jake arrived home at the same time I did. He'd been visiting his new girlfriend. He went into the kitchen to get something to drink. I went upstairs.

Music was blaring from Tasmin's room. There was a strong smell of dope. Her door was slightly ajar. She and Howard were sprawled on her bed, a tub of ice cream between them. I watched Howard dip his finger into the ice cream, and slowly bring it to Tasmin's lips. She giggled. He giggled. She sucked his finger. They never took their eyes off one another, not even as he scooped his hands back into the ice cream tub. He did it again, and again. She sucked his finger. And again. She brushed a strand of hair from her face. All in slow motion. And it was the way they looked at one another.

Jake was standing beside me. He put his hand on my shoulder.

'She was smoking the joint when I came in,' Howard said. 'I never gave it to her.'

'It's not the dope, and you know it.'

'I don't know what you're talking about.'

'Hey, what happened to my Glenfiddich?' Howard asks.

I refill my rapidograph and adjust the set square. 'Your rollerblades are in the front closet,' I say. 'I forgot to put them out with the rest of your things. Or are those Jake's?'

'They're Jake's.' Howard comes over to the drafting table. 'What's this?'

'A renovation. The wife has MS. They need to make the house wheelchair friendly.'

'Oh.' He points to the lipstick-knife. 'I meant this.'

'The picture? Just something I found in a magazine.'

He frowns. 'What's it for?'

'No clue. D'you need a hand carrying stuff to your car?'

One summer, when I was still married to Lars, we took a trip to Italy. In the Museo dell'Opera del Duomo, in Florence, we marvelled at the wooden models of Brunelleschi's Duomo, and at the gilded brass panels Ghiberti fashioned for the Baptistery 'Gates of Paradise' doors. And then we saw Michelangelo's *Pietà*.

The Florentine *Pietà* is massive – almost two and a half metres tall – and profoundly moving. The pathos of its four marble figures is extraordinary. They appear outwardly calm, but the statue crackles with psychic energy.

A young man was making a charcoal drawing of the sculpture in a large sketchbook. An elderly woman stood with hands clasped, lips moving in hushed prayer.

When Michelangelo began carving this sculpture, he was already old and sick. He intended it for his own tomb. The largest figure, of Nicodemus, who stands behind Christ, is a remarkably honest and poignant self-portrait of the artist as an old man.

Michelangelo laboured on this *Pietà* for ten years. Then one day he began to smash it with a sledgehammer. He broke off limbs and almost destroyed the sculpture entirely before a servant managed to restrain him.

An assistant eventually repaired the work. One of Christ's legs is still missing.

Who can make sense of that heartbreak? How can we imagine the heft of that sledgehammer in the old man's hands?

I roll up the drawings to show the Haydens in the morning, and pour myself the last of Howard's Glenfiddich.

Perhaps I'll put in a skylight over the staircase, convert the attic to an office, tear down some of these walls. I close my eyes. Planes shift and intersect, shafts of light are refracted through sheets of glass. Shapes hover in the periphery of my mind, insubstantial and insistent as dreams. They will come, slowly, and I will turn them over, shape them, give them form.

SEVEN MONTHS

Back when Meryl and Bruce first came to the city, lugging backpacks and Meryl's portfolio, they spent a couple of months staying with some people Bruce knew. They had to sleep in the basement on a thin piece of foam on the uneven concrete floor. The basement was filthy and dark as a cave, and until they got used to the racket they'd be jolted awake whenever the furnace fired up. The people they were staying with had two small children and their marriage was falling apart, so Meryl and Bruce would take the children outside while the parents yelled and wept through all the rooms of the house.

'We've got to get out of here,' Meryl said. She could no longer locate herself properly. She felt as if the things that circumscribed her life were becoming lost in the din and dark of that basement.

Eventually Bruce took a job reading gas meters and they found a cheap place for rent midtown, near the subway. It was the upper floor of a narrow brick semi on Alcorn Avenue. The landlady, whose name was Cora Leach, lived downstairs and when Meryl and Bruce went to look at the apartment she took her time coming to the door. She was a washed-out, tight-jawed woman with disappointed eyes. She stood aside to let them in, then her hands moved up slowly and pressed on her top-knotted paisley headscarf.

'You must excuse me,' she said, looking at Meryl. She kept her hands on her head and backed away. 'I need to fix my hair.' Her voice sounded as if she'd lived on cigarettes and gin for fifty years.

She hardly spoke again until after they'd walked through the apartment and agreed to rent it. She told them to leave the monthly cheque on the side table in the hallway, then she drifted towards the front door and folded her bony arms across her chest. 'And keep the screens on the windows,' she said. 'If a bat gets in, I'll scream.'

'If a *bat* gets in?' Bruce said as they left. He gave a high-pitched giggle. 'She's out of her tree.'

'Shh,' Meryl hissed, pulling her tuque over her ears. She looked back and the gap between the ground floor curtains closed.

The floors creaked badly and the place was dingy, with grime-streaked windows and slivers of paint and wood peeling off the frames, but there was a small room at the back that Meryl could use as a design studio, and there would be light and air and no furnace shuddering through their dreams.

First thing they did was paint – pale lemon walls, indigo trim. They bought some oversized cushions, a foam mattress, a second-hand drawing board, a spider plant. They made brick-and-plank bookshelves and got Bruce's mother to send his psychology texts. They tacked Polaroids and postcards to the fridge and around the bathroom mirror. They lit candles and ate on the floor, reclining against the cushions like Romans.

In the front hallway were two doors: straight ahead was the door leading upstairs to their apartment, and to the right was Cora Leach's door, with the thermostat on the far side of it. All winter they'd creep downstairs and turn the thermostat up, then they'd check their watches to see how long it took for Cora Leach to turn it back down. They had their own doorbell, which seldom rang, and when it did it was usually the ginseng salesman. They'd invite him up and the three of them would sit on the floor, smoking cigarettes and listening to J.J. Cale or Tim Buckley while they sipped mugs of ginseng tea. The salesman said ginseng worked wonders for your sex life. He was a robust Dane who had the habit of pausing mid-sentence with his eyes closed as if he were seeking solace.

Occasionally the doorbell rang during the day, but when Meryl went downstairs it was the Meals on Wheels volunteer to visit Cora Leach, who'd been slower than usual getting to the door. Meryl retreated quickly, unsettled by the volunteer's cheerfulness.

Meryl had trouble getting out of bed that winter. Every day she slept a little later. When she finally dragged herself up, she'd pull on her boots and head out to the store at the end of the street for cigarettes and a newspaper. Then she'd make coffee and sit at her drawing board, scanning the want ads and idly circling jobs she had no

intention of applying for. She managed to get the odd freelance
assignment – a toy package design, a restaurant menu, the T-shirts
for a morticians' convention – and she toyed with an idea for a children's pop-up book. She took long baths, submerged up to her ears
in water so hot her skin turned red, while she listened to her skull
vibrate as she hummed a sustained note, or stared at the damp patch
that had discoloured a corner of the bathroom ceiling. Most afternoons she'd fall asleep and emerge hours later from strange half-
dreams, like a small bubble rising through oil, adrift and vaguely
nauseated in the gathering dusk. Sometimes when she looked out the
front window she'd see Cora Leach in her paisley headscarf and
cat's-eye sunglasses, clutching a couple of bottles in paper bags and
moving down the street with long, low strides, toe-to-heel, her
skinny hips thrust forward.

Bruce would come back at night with the cold still clinging to
him, the thick smell of clammy wool and damp leather on his hair
and hands. He kicked off his boots and his smile had the edge of a
grimace. Meryl waited for him to ask what she'd done all day, to
demand evidence of productivity – pop-up lizards or company logos
or fresh-baked brownies – but he never did, and she was beginning
to hate him.

After that long drawl of winter was over, Meryl stood on the sidewalk
and blinked, smitten with the throbbing sunlight. Tiny leaves on the
tree at the edge of the cramped yard unfurled like hopeful fists, and
houses were being renovated up and down the street. Cement mixers
and carpenters came and went.

She walked for hours, breathing deep, her pores opening to the
warmth. When she got back to the house, cradling strawberries or a
pot of ink or a new book, she'd glimpse the quick pale smudge of fingers or a face between the drapes on Cora Leach's window.

One brilliant spring day she brought a volume of Chekhov outside and sprawled in a patch of sunlight in the front yard. The sun
was hot on her bare legs and the new grass smelled sweet. When she
looked up from her book a small plane was crawling across the sky,

trailing a banner that read *Marry Me Donna*. The guy carrying two-by-fours into the house next door smiled at her and she smiled back and stretched her toes and remembered what happiness felt like.

She told herself it was the sunshine, the balmy breeze that brought her out there again with her book the following morning. She glanced up from time to time, fiddling with the hem of her white muslin sundress. When he finally emerged in the neighbour's garden, a tool-belt slung low across his hips, he spread his arms wide and called out, 'So beautiful,' grinning in a way that made her unsure whether he was referring to the weather or to her.

His name was Eric and he was renovating the adjacent house for new owners who hadn't moved in yet. After he and Meryl had exchanged pleasantries outside for a week or two, he invited her in to see how he was transforming the place. He ushered her through unfinished rooms, steering her around planks and exposed joists and screws. 'Amazing,' she said, standing in the shafted light of the master bed-room.

They sat in the bay window upstairs. 'Look,' she said, leaning out. 'You can see my window from here.' Eric smiled slowly, held her gaze until she looked away. He took a joint out of his tool-belt, lit it and passed it to her, his hand brushing against hers and lingering briefly. After a couple of tokes she asked if she could stay a while and watch him work.

Meryl thought he looked too young to know so many remarkable things. He could trace fingertips over blueprints and translate the simple intersection of lines into skylights and staircases and vaulted ceilings. He understood how weather caused wood to heave and mortar to crack and basements to flood, and when he planed a door-jamb his palm swept across the grain with the ease of a violinist.

Smooth and even, she thought as he drilled and measured and sanded. *No jagged bits.*

The next day Eric came over to use the phone. She made tea while he rolled a joint, and twenty minutes later he had his tongue down her throat and she was tugging off her jeans and inhaling the hot sawdust-and-musk smell of his hair.

Meryl first became aware of the noise a moment before she climaxed.

'What the hell *is* that?' Eric gasped.

It was a steady pounding, vibrating the floor directly beneath them. Eric rolled off her. Meryl squinted, trying to bring him into focus. She had the stoned notion that he was a figment, the sticky residue of sleep.

The pounding stopped. Meryl sighed. 'It's the landlady,' she said, and then she started to laugh.

That evening Bruce stood with his back to her at an open kitchen cupboard and quietly announced, 'It's all over.'

Meryl's heart sank so fast she almost collapsed. She thought of the traces of Eric that must still linger on the floorboards and walls and under her fingernails. She thought of Cora Leach banging a broomstick on the ceiling. Then Bruce shook his head and said, 'Fucking mouse shit everywhere.'

He opened and closed cupboard doors. He peered behind the fridge and under the sink. 'We better get some traps,' he said. 'You want to take care of it?'

Meryl had to bite her lower lip to make herself stop nodding. 'Sure,' she said, her voice high and slightly out of tune.

The next morning Meryl woke up early, squeezed her eyes shut and thought, *I won't go to him.* She swept the floor and wiped mouse droppings off the shelves. She sat at her drawing board and thought about the way Eric's shoulders moved when he sanded wood and how he looked at her, with a slow blink and the lazy beginning of a smile that made her want to shiver and bellow at the same time. She went down the stairs as if someone had spun her around, aimed her in that direction and shoved, and when she opened the front door he was already there, his finger reaching for the doorbell.

This time the banging on the ceiling below them began almost immediately and became more urgent as their lovemaking progressed. They moaned and whooped and thudded back with feet and hands.

That night Meryl and Bruce baited traps with bits of cheddar, and set them behind the fridge and next to the toaster and on the shelf beside the Froot Loops. Meryl hoped they wouldn't catch the mouse. She had no idea what she would do with its soft broken body.

I'm in too deep, Meryl thought as she pressed her cheek against Eric's hairless chest and he told her things about himself. He was allergic to asparagus. The year after high school he'd worked on the crew of a charter sailing around the Caribbean. He played slide guitar. He'd spent boyhood summers helping his grandfather build houses up around Lake Simcoe. When he was sixteen his mother had sat in her car in the locked garage one afternoon with the engine running and five bags of groceries on the back seat, and by the time they found her the ice cream had melted over the upholstery. His dog, a three-legged black lab named Blue, liked to sleep with the loose folds of her throat on his feet. Eric's nostrils flexed and a tiny muscle twitched under his eye, and Meryl thought, *Way too deep.*

She told him mice were getting in. She was convinced there must be more than one. Maybe an entire mouse family was living in that apartment. She'd heard them scrabbling in the garbage and skittering like dislodged secrets across the floor, and there were fresh droppings in the closet and on the soap. One night she'd opened her eyes to find a little mouse face staring at her in the darkness for a moment before it scurried away.

Eric shrugged. 'All they need is a hole as thin as a pencil. Set some traps.'

'We did. They don't work.'

'What did you use for bait?'

'Cheese.'

'Cheese? They hate cheese.'

'Mice love cheese.'

'In cartoons maybe. Try peanut butter.'

Meryl lit a cigarette. After Eric left she gouged peanut butter from the jar and, with trembling fingers, reset the traps.

Meryl and Bruce bought a seventeen-inch TV and watched sitcoms and ball games and old movies for hours.

'What happened to the ginseng salesman?' Bruce asked one night during a commercial break. 'I miss that guy.'

It was a muggy night. All the windows were open wide. Meryl said, 'Must've gone back to Denmark. He was homesick.'

After work that day Bruce had sat at Meryl's drawing board, his mouth a grim scribble, updating his résumé and addressing envelopes.

'It's pretty pathetic,' he said, staring at the flickering TV screen while a woman poured blue liquid over a disposable diaper, 'when all you've got is the ginseng salesman. He never even said goodbye.'

A couple of hours later Meryl lay awake and thought, *What happens when he leaves?* She kicked free of the twisted sheet and looked at Bruce. He was sleeping on his side with his arms bent in front of his face as if he were warding off a blow. His breath made strangled watery sounds. Meryl wondered what he dreamed about. *Even when he sleeps he's folded tight*, she thought.

'I'm behind schedule,' Eric said one morning. 'They want to move in at the end of the month.'

He told Meryl he probably couldn't see her for a few days. New windows were being delivered, someone would be helping him drywall ceilings, and he'd arranged to pick up the kitchen tiles.

The next afternoon the doorbell rang. Meryl rushed downstairs and fumbled with the knob, but it was only the Meals on Wheels volunteer.

'Sorry to bother you,' she said cheerfully. 'There's no answer downstairs.'

Meryl let her in. The volunteer knocked on Cora Leach's door a couple of times. She shifted her weight back and forth, smiled at

Meryl, cleared her throat and shouted, 'Hello? Anybody home?' She waited a moment, then rapped on the door again. 'Well,' she said, glancing doubtfully at her watch, 'I guess I'll come back later.'

Meryl followed her out and stood on the sidewalk alongside Eric's van. She watched the next-door house for a while but there was no sign of Eric, so she went back inside.

A couple of days later Bruce asked, 'Have you seen Cora Leach lately?'

'I don't think so. No, not for a while. Why?'

'The rent cheque's been on the table downstairs since Tuesday. And there's mail for her,' he said. 'I can't believe you didn't notice.'

Meryl shrugged. 'Maybe she's gone on holiday. Or drunk herself into a stupor.' Then she remembered the Meals on Wheels volunteer.

'We should call the police,' Bruce said.

Ten minutes later a cruiser pulled up front and two large policemen got out. They hitched up their trousers in unison and walked slowly towards the front door. Meryl hugged herself while Bruce explained the situation to them.

One of the policemen hammered on Cora Leach's door. 'Ma'am?' he called. He tried the knob, then turned to Meryl and Bruce. 'You folks have a spare key?'

They shook their heads. 'We're just the tenants,' Bruce said.

'She keeps to herself,' Meryl added quickly. 'She doesn't want company. She's pretty much made that clear.'

The policeman gave her a blank look, then he sniffed and turned his attention back to the door. He appeared to have taken charge. His partner just stood there and watched as he removed some sort of lock-picking device from his pocket, inserted it into the lock and jiggled it around. After a while he looked at his partner and sighed.

'Okay,' the other cop told Meryl and Bruce. 'Stand aside.' It was the first time he'd spoken. He had a surprisingly squeaky voice for a large man.

Meryl and Bruce took a couple of steps backwards. The lock-picking policeman motioned with his hand that they should move farther away. 'You folks better wait outside,' he told them. There was a loud thud and then a splintering sound as he kicked the door.

Meryl and Bruce waited out on the front walk while the two policemen investigated.

'It's like a movie,' Meryl said.

'These clowns seem to think so,' Bruce muttered.

Meryl glanced at the house next door. The windows were closed and Eric's van was gone. 'Shit,' she said. 'What if she's dead?'

'She's probably been dead for days. That renovation's taking a long time.'

'What?'

'Next door. Should have been done by now. Seems like a nice guy, though.'

Meryl felt herself blush. 'Who?'

'The builder.'

'Oh, you met him?'

'Yeah.'

'He say anything?'

'About what?'

'I don't know. About when he'll be finished. Or the new neighbours.'

'Not really.'

She waited until she trusted herself to speak again, then motioned towards Cora Leach's window. 'I wonder what's going on in there.'

Eventually the lock-picking policeman came outside.

'Is she okay?' Bruce asked.

The policeman stood in front of them with his thumbs hooked under his belt. 'Yep. The lady's fine.'

'Is she in there?' Meryl asked.

'No ma'am. We found out she's been in the hospital since Monday. There was a bottle of medication next to her bed so we managed to contact the doctor.'

'Ah,' Bruce said, nodding.

'They're discharging her tomorrow.'

'Great,' Meryl said.

'We thought she was dead,' Bruce explained.

The glimmer of a smile appeared briefly on the policeman's face. 'Nah. You would've smelled her by now.'

Bruce grinned. 'Never thought of that.'

The policeman pushed his tongue along his gums to remove bits of food stuck between his teeth. He shook his head. 'Something I don't understand,' he said.

'What's that?' Bruce asked.

'You folks lived here long?'

'Uh – seven, eight months,' Bruce replied. 'Why?'

'You say this lady, this Mrs Leach? She lives alone?'

'That's right.'

He rubbed his hand slowly back and forth over his crew cut. 'You never saw anyone else? Nobody coming or going?'

'Only the woman from Meals on Wheels,' Meryl answered. 'She's a bit of a recluse. Mrs Leach, I mean.'

'So you had no idea about the old gentleman?'

'The old gentleman?' Bruce repeated.

'*Mis*ter Leach.' The policeman sighed. 'You see, what I'm wondering is how you could live upstairs all this time and not know he was in there.'

Bruce exhaled with a long whistling sound. 'Wow. I'm stunned. I'm totally stunned.'

Meryl shook her head. 'We really had no idea.'

'Not a clue,' Bruce said.

The policeman frowned. He looked at them, then at the house, then back at them. 'All right,' he said. 'We'll file a report. There's no point uprooting him now if the wife's getting back tomorrow. Can you check in on him? The old guy can't see.'

'Sure,' Meryl promised. 'We'll look in on him.'

Bruce rapped on the kicked-in door. 'Sir?' he said loudly. 'We're the tenants, from upstairs.'

The drapes were drawn and the room smelled like stale air and body odour. Dust motes floated in the gloom.

'Nothing wrong with my hearing,' the old man replied. He was sitting on a stained maroon armchair. A mug half-filled with ancient coagulated coffee was on the small table beside him, and pieces of potato chips and corn flakes littered the worn oriental rug at his feet. He was wearing mismatched socks with holes around the big toes, his shirt was filthy and he had scraggly shoulder-length grey hair.

Bruce stepped up to the old man and extended his hand. 'I'm Bruce, and this is my wife Meryl. How're you doing?'

'Eh,' the old man replied, scrunching his face and staring straight ahead. He kept his hands on the armrests. There was a livid bruise on his forearm, and his fingernails were dirty and badly in need of trimming.

Meryl tried not to breathe too deeply. The smell was horrible. 'Glad to meet you,' she said.

Meryl returned later with a plate of lasagna and salad for the old man. While he ate, she tidied. She opened windows, washed dishes and spoons, threw away half-eaten cans of tuna and spaghetti, wiped counters and tables and vacuumed the floor. When she finished cleaning she went to remove her plate from the old man's lap.

'I'll take that if you're finished, Mr Leach.'

He scowled and held onto the plate. Meryl tugged it gently.

'Hussy,' he whispered fiercely, then he let go. His mouth opened to reveal discoloured teeth and his shoulders shook with silent laughter.

Meryl's cheeks were still burning when she went upstairs. Afterwards she thought that perhaps she'd misheard. Maybe he'd said 'lassie'.

'The place was an absolute pigsty,' Meryl told Bruce.

'I don't know why you bothered. What a waste of energy,' he replied. He was writing more job applications.

'I felt sorry for him. And her. Nobody wants to get out of hospital and walk into a pigsty.'

'It's always like that. Guaranteed. Did you take a good look at him? The guy's half blind and nobody cuts his hair or tells him his pants are ripped.'

They heard a mousetrap spring in the kitchen.

'Aha!' Bruce jumped up. 'Finally! We got one!'

'I'm not going near it,' Meryl said.

Bruce went to check. When he came back he looked disappointed. 'False alarm. It got away.'

'But why? Why would she neglect him like that? It's like he's a prisoner down there.'

Bruce shrugged. 'She's a crazy old lush. She can barely take care of herself.'

'No,' Meryl said. 'No, that's not it. I think she's punishing him for something. He must have done something terrible.'

Bruce shrugged again, and went back to working on his job applications. Without looking up, he said, 'You know, those mice are getting totally out of hand. The traps are useless. Who told you to use peanut butter?'

'I don't remember. I must've read it somewhere.'

Bruce scratched his jaw and raised his eyebrows. 'Really? Well, it's not working. I think we need poison. Will you get some?'

Meryl sighed. 'I guess.'

When Meryl got back from the store with a box of poison a couple of days later, Cora Leach was standing in the hallway.

'How are you?' Meryl asked.

'I'm fine, thank you,' Cora Leach replied. She was examining her door and her expression was grim. 'This door needs fixing.'

'I'm sorry,' Meryl said. 'That was the police. We were worried.' Through the open door she could see Mr Leach shuffling around. He shook his head in their direction and waved his arms in a gesture of dismissal, or hopelessness.

'It'll cost a pretty penny,' Cora Leach said.

Eric came back and they made love on the living-room floor to the percussive broomstick accompaniment beneath them.

'Back to normal,' Meryl murmured.

'I have to get going,' he said. 'It's looking good next door. I'm almost finished.'

'And then what?' Meryl asked.

He stared at the ceiling. 'I don't know.'

She got up, went over to the window, and felt her jaw drop. Cora Leach was out there, walking towards the house with her liquor store bags.

Eric came up from behind and wrapped his arms around Meryl. 'That your landlady?' he asked.

'Uh-huh,' she answered slowly.

It was almost midnight when Meryl went to investigate the sounds from the kitchen. She stood in the doorway and gave a tiny scream. A mouse was writhing in an agonized death dance in the middle of the kitchen floor. It squealed as its small body jerked spasmodically and its tail whipped the linoleum.

'It's the poison,' Bruce said quietly. He was standing beside her. 'They die of thirst.'

'Please do something,' Meryl whispered.

Bruce fetched one of his winter boots. He eyed the squirming mouse, then brought the boot down hard on its rear end and jumped back. Meryl winced and covered her mouth with her hand. 'Oh God,' she moaned. Bruce glanced at her, his mouth curled in disgust. The mouse's tail flicked and its foreleg quivered. Bruce raised the boot, and when he bashed the twitching mouse he uttered the same triumphant grunt he gave during the final thrust and shudder of sex. The broomstick thumped on the ceiling below them.

'You believe that?' he said. 'She's banging on the fucking ceiling.'

He pounded the mouse again, and again, and each time the broomstick rapped its response. His features looked wildly disorganized. 'Crazy bitch,' he yelled.

He kept on bashing at the remnants of the mouse. Bits of fur and blood stuck to the sole of his boot, and a rivulet of perspiration ran down his forehead. He stood taut-limbed like an avenging street fighter in the middle of the kitchen and stared at the pulpy red mess of the pulverized mouse. 'Fuck you,' he gasped.

He raised his arm again, but Meryl caught it on the upswing and held on. 'It's not her,' she sobbed, pulling him close. 'It was him.'

She kept on holding him. She fell asleep like that, holding him tight, and she was still holding on to him when she woke up next morning.

COLLEEN, THROUGH THE WINDOW

'I told her, you can't expect to get off scot-free.'

If Colleen were out on the front lawn (the grass needs cutting) or even the sidewalk, she'd be able to hear her mother's rasping voice carrying all the way from the open living-room window.

'That's why she's here. Can't go back to her husband. She left three kids. What does she expect?'

Colleen is alone in her mother's kitchen, making a fresh pot of coffee. Gladys McCarthy, an ex-neighbour who moved away years ago, is visiting.

'Running off like a love-crazed fool.'

Colleen stands at the kitchen sink.

Out the window and back almost thirty years there's little Colleen in the apple tree, humming in the crook of a branch, rough bark scraping her plump legs. She is waiting for the Perfect Moment, when Mrs McCarthy will peer over the fence or her father will wave from the kitchen window or a wind will rustle through the leaves or a whiff of sweet hot grass will reach her wrinkling nose, and then she'll grab the branch with both hands, slip down and swing, her fingers gripping tight, legs kicking higher and higher, way up into the sky. She holds her breath, suspended for a moment at the highest point, then releases her grasp and flies.

If someone were looking through Colleen's bedroom window back when she was sixteen, seventeen, eighteen, they would see nothing (except maybe a pack of smokes or a roach-clip left on the windowsill). The drapes are drawn.

They wouldn't have seen T-shirts ripped off, jeans unzipped and flung aside, panties slipped down, Colleen and Wayne slithering and sliding and humping on the bed, quick, before her mother got home. Sometimes at night when the family had gone to bed they'd even do it in the living room, on the carpet beside the ottoman. That's how she learned to be silent, bite her lip, claw and scratch while the hot breath bunched in her throat but quiet, don't let anyone hear. Years later Tom told her he hated that she never squealed and moaned with passion or cried out like women in movies, but then there were children to be quiet from.

Wayne had this walk, like he'd just climbed off his motorbike and could still feel the metal straddled between his legs – thumbs looped into the back pockets of his jeans, shoulders back, pelvis forward, swaying. One side of his mouth lifted in a grin; one eyebrow raised.

She'd ride behind him, his hair whipping back caught between her teeth, the warm hardness of his legs gripped between her thighs, her hands around his waist, the engine vibrating.

Nobody could have seen Colleen in the bathroom (frosted panes so not even Mrs McCarthy could spy from next door), her skin scarlet, submerged in the hottest bath water she could stand, or pummelling her belly, or jumping off the toilet seat over and over (her mother yelling *Colleen what the hell's going on in there?* through the locked door). And then her period, finally, ten days late.

Young Colleen, a bruised peach. A large girl, never quite neat, brown hair lanky, mottled skin that marks easily with bursts of purples and reds and yellows (*a careless girl*, her mother would say, *always knocking into things*).

Colleen winds down the car window. She is a stunned puff of white; her wedding veil foams and billows and itches around hairsprayed curls. She is floating on the smiles of the crowd surrounding the car. Tom is laughing, leaning across from the driver's seat beside her. His tie is undone and his cheek is smeared with lipstick. She met him on a double-date with Veronica, her maid of honour. She has known him for eight months. He sells life insurance.

Wayne was not invited to her wedding. She hasn't seen him for a couple of years. Last she heard, he'd moved out East somewhere. She's angry with him, but she doesn't remember why.

She whips her arm through the car window and her bouquet

soars up, ribbons streaking, a blur of white suspended for a moment at its highest point then tumbling towards waving fingers.

Colleen, moving past her kitchen window, is trying to keep on top of things. Hair a mess, livid bags under her eyes, a dribble of red wine and a spatter of oil that won't wash out on the front of her sweat-shirt. Under her sweats her shins and forearms are bruised (still careless, still bumping into things). The kids spilling, pinching, sulk-ing, whining, and she snaps, her voice shrilling like the kettle. Tom sits welded to the TV, shouting could they please keep it down. And here she is, thirty-four years old, mute and meek as the kids' rabbit, pink-rimmed eyes and twitchy nose and drooping ears, stuck in this stifling hutch of a life where the colours are all wrong, the edges dull.

Tom has yawned and farted and burped beery breath for so long she doesn't care that they edge by one another, colliding from time to time, blunt tongues suddenly sharp. And why would he love her? She's all folded in on herself, bunches of bright veins on her bruised legs and rutted white marks mapped across her squashed breasts. But what makes her hate him is his coiled anger: she sees it in the way he can't resist a mirror, preening (not for her, she knows), comb-ing and patting his hair over the spreading bald spot, hulking for-ward towards the mirror. The way he scowls, glowering, hands on thrust-forward hips, elbows out. As he practises his glower (and how well she knows it, this tight-spun look as he breathes out between his teeth, *Why didn't you call the TV repairman There's nothing to eat in this house Why is there no fucking soap*) she looks at his reflection and back at him and thinks, My God there's two of them, two of him, then it occurs to her that she would be extremely happy if the glow-ering reflection would step out from the bathroom mirror and the two of them, man and mirror-man, each smoothing his hair back, would have a showdown, menace shouldering against menace, until they cancel one another out.

She sits at the kitchen table unable to move, everything – blood, breath, the blinking of her eyes – slowed down; the sounds – squab-bling kids, blaring TV – stretched out to a throbbing drone. She watches the sun glint through the window and light up the dust on the pane where the kids blow moist fogs of breath then scribble their names with grubby fingertips; she sits with the steam coming off her coffee and the late-day sun sliding rose and gold over her face and down her arm.

Colleen is watching from the window of a coffee shop as Wayne walks across the street. The same strut, except instead of a Harley he's pulled up in a white Chevrolet. He's thicker around the belly, his face is fleshier and his hair's thinned, like Tom's.

She recognized the voice right away when he called. The way he said *Colleen*, so gruff and sweet, she'd almost dropped the phone.

He walks through the door with the same cockeyed grin and her throat, her knees, her sagging heart become pulsing liquid.

Two hours later she lies pressed against him in a motel room and cries. When he tries to console her she tells him it's not sadness or guilt – she's crying because she realizes how she's been holding her breath.

Colleen, looking out at the apple tree, is startled when her mother yells, 'Hey, Colleen, d'you get lost? What's happened to our coffee?'

She's arranged to visit her children on Sunday. They'll probably be tearful, or awkward, pockets of clumsy silences will pile up between them. Curious too, because their mother came so close to death, she sat right beside it.

She could tell them that after you've slammed against death there's nothing to be afraid of ever again, but that wouldn't be true.

There are whispers at the supermarket and the bus stop. They're all thinking (Gladys McCarthy too; Colleen sees it in her eyes): How tragic, to be given another shot at living happily ever after with your one true love and then to lose everything. They're whispering, Isn't fate strange: he's killed outright; she escapes with nothing more serious than a few bruises and a broken arm. Saved by an airbag. Only one, on the driver's side. Wouldn't you just want to die?

Through the windows (insect- and mud-spattered) of Wayne's Chevrolet, farmhouses fields hills stream by. Colleen pushes a strand of hair from her face with one hand, holds the steering wheel steady with the other. They've been on the road for three days, heading west. She squints through her sunglasses, lowers the visor against the glare of the late-afternoon sun, sprays wiper fluid on the windshield. Dust and insects smear together in streaks of pale brown.

Wayne turns up the radio: U2, thumping 'With or Without You'. He sings along but he gets most of the words wrong and has trouble hitting high notes.

He uncaps a bottle of Southern Comfort, takes a swig, wipes the top and hands it to her, his raised eyebrow lifting even higher. She shakes her head.

'C'mon,' he says, 'don't be such a downer.' He starts complaining about his ex-wife and alimony payments. His fingers thrum on the dashboard as he spits out insults. When they get settled out West he's going to send for his little girl. He figures he can get custody because his ex-wife's psychotic, any judge'll see that. Plus he coached Little League – that'll be points in his favour.

'You better stop drinking.' Colleen says. 'There's no way I'm doing all the driving.'

'Well, aren't we in a pissy mood.' He leans over and kisses her neck, his breath sloppy on her ear.

She shrugs him off, 'Cut it out, Wayne.'

Last night she lay awake on a motel bed trying to stop the slow terrible throb in her head. Car headlights swept over their bodies, Wayne's arm stretched across her chest, and she wanted to tear off her skin.

She fixes her eyes on the yellow line that divides the two-lane. She's being dragged along by this seamless rope of a line; she could go on driving forever and never reach the end of it. She'd still be on the same road with the same yellow line stretching on and on and on.

A horn sounds – an oncoming pickup.

'Jesus, Colleen, get back in your lane – you're driving in the middle of the road.'

She can't stop thinking about her kids, wondering whether they'll remember to bring money to school for next week's field trip. She pictures them blinking in the darkness of their bedrooms, lying with the covers pulled up over their ears. And Tom: finding the note she left, sitting for hours staring at the floor, not even watching TV, all that anger finally uncoiled into a long hushed loneliness.

'We should pull over at the next town, get something to eat. I need to take a leak,' Wayne says. He looks in the side mirror, pulls out his comb and sleeks his hair back. 'The guy behind us is trying to pass. Slow down, let him go by.'

It's as if someone has poured mud into the top of her head and it's spread to her ears, her throat, the pit of her belly. She can't speak; she may never be able to speak again.

She presses harder on the accelerator. The yellow line streaks on, doubled now as the road curves. She checks the mirror – the car behind has dropped back.

'For Chrissakes, Colleen, slow down!'

She rounds the bend, gives more gas. Up ahead a car is straddling the centre line, overtaking a tractor-trailer.

'What the fuck are you doing? He's going to hit us!'

Wayne grabs the wheel but Colleen holds on, hands gripping tight. She floors the accelerator. Horns are screaming; they're surging towards the car that's the end of the yellow line. Head steady, eyes straight ahead, then just before they collide she turns the wheel, hard. She holds her breath; blood whistles in her ears as they swerve off the road and they're flying, the Chevrolet spinning and hurtling down an embankment. They slam into a tree, the door on Wayne's side is ripped off, the windshield shatters, the car hisses and drips, and Colleen is ballooned, stunned, in an airbag.

Colleen brings the fresh pot of coffee to the living room and pours refills. Gladys McCarthy pats her hand, 'Thank you, dear.' Colleen lowers her eyes.

She cuts herself a large piece of cake.

Her mother sighs, lights another cigarette. Smoke spumes from her nostrils. 'She's got a part-time job at a video store. Pays a pittance. Hardly enough for her food here. I keep telling her, she better take a course in computers or something.'

Colleen scoops cake crumbs into her mouth. She looks out the window. Her mother's Toyota is parked out front.

'Is it okay if I take your car? We're almost out of milk. I better get some – it's getting late.'

'The key's in my purse,' her mother says. 'And buy me a carton of smokes.' As Colleen walks down the hallway her mother says to Gladys, 'I thought she'd be dead scared of driving after the accident, but she's okay.'

Colleen finds the key and $170 in her mother's wallet.

She gets into the Toyota and starts the engine. Almost a full tank of gas – she won't have to stop for at least three or four hours. She opens the windows, breathes in deep and roars as she pulls away, drowning in so much air, the rose-spread sky that goes on and on.

ORANGE BUOYS

The old man drives down the dirt road past some shacks and coconut palms to where the road peters out and beach begins. He parks in the shade alongside the fishing boat that a couple of men have been working on for the past few months.

It's the heat of the day. It's always the heat of the day when he comes down here.

The boat-builders stop their hammering and planing for a moment to exchange greetings with him. Calypso blares from the boom box on their workbench.

He walks along the beach with a careful old-man's shuffle, the skin loose on his ribs and thighs. Past the beached dory some bright spark has rechristened 'Titanic', and the clumps of oiled tourists roasting on towels, to where the bay is smoothest, rock-free.

Horace and Winston are already here, bobbing in the bay – old men like him, but locals, not transplants from northern cities.

'Ah, you here at las',' Winston calls. 'De Director.'

The old man grins and waves as he makes his bent-kneed way to the water's edge, and wades in, humming softly.

They call him the Director even though he never was director of anything. Director of this beach. He's been coming here for more than sixteen years, day after day, even if it rains. Because you get wet anyway.

'Hot today,' he says when he reaches them.

'Yes,' Horace says. 'Very hot.'

'It is,' agrees Winston.

Winston's granddaughter is becoming a hematologist, in Boston. She'll be home in a couple of weeks for Christmas. Horace doesn't want to think about Christmas because he still misses his wife with a raw, blinking, chin-jutting grief. She'll be dead a year this April.

The old man's wife is dead too. There are sons and grandsons who fly down for brief visits from time to time, but mostly he's alone.

He stands so that the surge of the water breaks on his chest, and hums tunelessly to himself. Then he tilts his tanned face to the sun, closes his eyes, and listens to the sweep and sigh of the sea.

They stay in the sea for an hour, an hour and a half, day after day. Talking about the weather in New York or Calgary or London. Where the blizzards are; which airports are closed; wind-chill equivalents. They chuckle and sigh in the thick lush heat. They discuss the damage from last week's floods, the candidates for the election, and how you get Miz Pringle to save you her choice fish.

'Bottle o' rum,' Horace says. 'Works bes' wi' she.'

Vacationing children shout and splash around them; jet-skis cut across the bay; nubile young women adjust tiny bikinis as they emerge, soaked and sun-dazzled, from the water.

'My oh my,' the old man says, and gives a long, soft whistle. 'Swim on over, darling. Oh yes. Just look at the curves on that little beauty.'

Fat swift clouds roll across the sky periodically, then the sun blazes through again.

'De family lef' yet?' Horace asks.

'They go this evening,' the old man answers. 'They're late today. Must be packing.'

For the past two weeks his great-niece and her family have joined them in the sea. They've rented a villa nearby, and the old man has been invited over for a few meals. This evening they'll fly back to Philadelphia. The old man is fond of this young niece – she's a lively woman with an easy, open laugh. She and her husband and two small boys have brought the husband's younger sister along with them on vacation, to cheer her up – she's miserable about a love affair that ended badly. Throughout the vacation she's been distracted and quiet. Uninterested in the attentions of the men on the beach. She reads and swims and plays with the little boys.

'Here dey come,' Horace says. 'Can' miss de final swim.'

Inflatable armbands are tugged onto the boys' skinny arms and they splash towards the old man with flapping, jerky strokes. He lunges at them, laughing, and tickles them. The boys giggle and squeal. He grabs one, hugs the squirming boy close, then lifts him up and roars as he tosses him into the sea. The boy sputters and gasps as he surfaces. 'More!' he yells, delighted.

'Now me!' the other demands, and as the old man raises him high out of the water he recalls playing this game with his own sons and grandsons, long ago, their sudden weight surprising as he held them aloft.

'All packed?' the old man asks when the boys tire of the game.

'Almost,' the niece says. 'Just the last few things. But we couldn't get Sara on our flight. It's overbooked. She's confirmed on tomorrow's plane, though. She'll have to stay at a hotel tonight.'

'Don't put her in a hotel,' the old man says. 'She can stay with me. There's plenty of room.'

Sara, the girl, is pale-eyed, fine-boned, freckled from the sun. She looks doubtful. 'It'll be much easier if I stay near the airport.'

'Nonsense,' he says. 'Why spend money on a hotel? I'll drive you up to my place, we'll have a nice dinner, and we'll come here for a swim tomorrow. You can take a taxi to the airport.'

'Are you sure? That's really kind of you.' She's suddenly beautiful when she smiles. She slips an elastic band off her wrist and ties her hair up. 'I'm off for a quick swim,' she says.

'Enjoy it while you can,' Winston says. 'You headin' back to snow. Chicago, New York. Eight inches in Buffalo yesterday.'

'But I still have another day,' she says, smiling again. Then she swims off, with quick strong strokes, clear across the bay.

'Thank you for inviting her,' the niece says. 'We felt awful about leaving her here alone.'

'I'm glad to have company.'

When the girl reaches the row of orange buoys at the far end of the bay, she turns around and begins swimming back.

'You hear dey gine tear down Heartsong?' Winston asks.

The old man might as well have been knocked flat by a rogue wave. 'Larissa's house?'

Winston nods. 'Buildin' a hotel.'

'Yes, I hear dat,' Horace says. 'Mus' be so.'

Larissa Lawson, Our Sweetheart of Song, left Hollywood and her
second husband when she was a star and came here, to the big house
at the end of this beach. She never went back. Never made another
movie or record, no matter who begged, or how much they offered.

She was here years before the old man came, long before they
called him the Director. He and his wife met her in the sea, and she
became their friend.

The orange buoys at the end of the bay are there because of him.
He petitioned government officials until they roped off an area so
Larissa could swim without being badgered by autograph hunters
and gawkers and water-ski boats. She'd swim every day, a slow, ele-
gant backstroke, riding the gentle swell, back and forth for almost
an hour, her pale arms sheathed in a long-sleeved leotard to protect
them from the sun.

Back when they first met, Arturo Moracci, the fashion designer,
had the villa next door to Larissa's, and a retired ambassador had
the place next to that. The parties they had in those three houses –
wonderful parties, night after night.

They're all gone now. Larissa died three years ago. But he still
talks to her. On heat-dazed afternoons, in the cemetery where she
and his wife are buried, he unspools his tight-wound secrets.

The old man spends the remainder of the afternoon with his niece's
family at their rented villa. When they leave for the airport, he drives
the girl Sara to his house.

He lives a couple of miles inland, on a hill, because of the cooler
breezes.

The girl admires his garden. He tells her it was much better
when his wife was alive – he hasn't the patience for it.

He puts a couple of bottles of wine in the refrigerator to chill. On
the way up he stopped to buy fish, and now he prepares it. He soaks
the fillets with sliced limes, then seasons them and rolls them in

breadcrumbs. He bakes sweet potatoes with pineapple, and fries plantains. The girl makes a salad.

After dinner they sit out on the veranda. 'It's paradise out here,' the girl says, closing her eyes and inhaling deeply. The wine seems to have relaxed her. She smiles often. She talks about the work she does for an environmental organization. He says all his sons are doctors – isn't that something – and then he remembers he has already told her this, probably a few times. He pours more wine and tells her how much this place has changed since he and his wife moved here – too many cars on the road now and prices sky high – and how Larissa Lawson sang for them at those wonderful parties of hers. The girl slowly strokes her arm and tilts her head as he speaks. When she stretches he can see the tips of her nipples through the flimsy fabric of her dress. The old man feels a little woozy. He fetches the framed picture of Larissa from the living room. The voice of an angel. She had real class. And what a shame that they're demolishing her house, because no hotel will ever match the liveliness and glamour and graciousness of Heartsong. He realizes his voice is too loud, he's almost shouting, so he shuts up for a moment and sits drumming his fingers on his knee.

'You remind me of her a little,' he says. 'Something about your eyes when you smile.'

The girl smiles and lowers her eyes. His fingertips graze her freckled shoulder as he offers her more wine, or a brandy, or some coffee perhaps, but she says she's fine. She crosses her long bare legs, smooths her silky dress over her thighs. She yawns, then yawns again.

'I'm sorry,' she says, shaking her head.

He takes her to the guest bedroom. Shows her the bathroom, the clean towels, and how to operate the ceiling fan. He removes the bedspread, plumps up the pillows, instructs her to leave the windows open wide, and the shutters, to get a breeze. And she should leave her door open.

'We've never closed doors or windows in this house. Not unless there's a big storm. You don't get neighbours breathing down your neck up here. Nobody around to bother you.'

After he says goodnight, he pours himself another glass of wine and goes back to the veranda. Fireflies flit and tango in the garden: sudden flares in the dark.

Larissa's third husband, a Swede, lasted five years, but there were always men lounging around Heartsong, their glistening young torsos bared to the sun, while she held court magnificently in the shade, coddling her creamy skin.

The old man clenches his jaw. Skin hunger, he thinks. It gnaws at you as bad as any other kind. He recalls an evening, about a month after his wife died, when he and Larissa sat under her gazebo, sipping martinis and watching as moonlight silvered the sea. Larissa's familiar perfume hung thick in the air. Her eyes, the softness of her skin, her laugh, were suddenly unbearably exquisite and he leaned over to kiss her, clumsily, the artery in his neck throbbing. She shook her head, and placed a gentle finger on his lips.

'You can't think straight, you're so full of grief,' she said.

He stumbled away soon after, and didn't go for his swim the next day, or the day after that.

On the third morning she phoned. 'Come for dinner tonight. Around seven-thirty.' She hung up before he could give an excuse, so he showed up at Heartsong at quarter to eight. And that was that.

The old man had spent hours at Larissa's bedside the weeks before she died. She'd gone slowly, but without complaint. There was so little left of her in the end that she barely made an indentation on the sheet.

He sits for a long time out on the veranda, thinking of Larissa, and of the girl. He wonders if she is sleeping yet, her long legs twisted around the bedclothes. 'Damn fool,' he says, and slams his fist hard on the table. Then he drains his glass, gets up, goes into the garden, and walks slowly around the house. He stops outside the guest room windows. She's closed the shutters.

The old man is there in the morning, pacing, when the girl unlocks the door. He has been there for hours. His head aches from the wine and lack of sleep.

She's carrying a toiletries bag and a towel. She's barefoot, wearing a skimpy T-shirt that has slipped off one shoulder. 'Hello,' she says.

Anger wells up, rushes through him, and he flies at her. 'How dare you!' he shouts, his face inches from hers. 'You'll do as you're told in my house!'

The girl recoils. 'I don't know what you mean,' she stammers.

'I told you – this door stays open. And the windows. And those shutters. Open, do you hear me?'

This anger is huge, and he has become huge with it. He wants to beat her, to bend her over and flog her. He spits words at her, and she winces. 'Just look at you. What man would even want you – flat-chested, no ass. Cover yourself. It makes me sick to see you.'

He is trembling uncontrollably. He feels as if his chest and throat might burst. The girl is on the verge of tears. 'Stop it,' she whispers.

He can't. Nothing will stop this rage. 'I know the sort of girl you are,' he snarls. 'No wonder your boyfriend left. You've got no shame. You'd go crawling right back into his bed if he'd take you.'

He watches her cower. And suddenly he feels better, feels the anger let go. He needs a cup of coffee. He leaves her standing there, gaping.

The girl is quiet while the old man drives down to the beach. He tries to draw her into conversation but she responds with barely audible monosyllables. She looks away, out the passenger window, or casts her eyes downward and twists her hands in her lap.

When they get out of the car, he greets the men who're building the boat.

'You have a beautiful girlfriend today,' one of them says, and winks at the girl. 'You beware o' dis man, darlin'. He gine break your heart.' The men laugh uproariously at this joke.

She is subdued in the sea. She watches the horizon.

'You sad to be leavin' us?' Horace asks.

The girl shrugs; barely smiles. She goes for a long swim. She reaches the row of orange buoys, ducks under the rope and keeps going, all the way to the rocks at the end of the pier. When she gets back she's shivering. She lies on her back on the beach, chest heaving, and closes her eyes.

The old man bobs with the waves. He moves his arms in slow circles through the water and counts out loud. He floats and watches the clouds. When the girl comes back into the sea, he hears Winston ask her if she's feeling all right. 'De ol' man interfere wi' you?'

She shrugs and looks down, her mouth shut tight, then she dives underwater and swims away.

As soon as they get back to his house, the girl goes off to take a shower. When she emerges from the bathroom, towelling her damp hair, it begins again. Reason slips away, and the rage takes hold of him. He hurls insults at her, yells at her, tells her she is disgusting and useless and what man would ever want her.

The girl is in tears. 'Why are you doing this? What did I do?'

She insists on calling a taxi. She'll leave early, and wait at the airport.

'I'll drive you there,' he says.

But she gathers her things and goes.

When the girl has left, the old man feels terribly tired. He lies on the couch and sinks into a brief, uneasy doze, until something – his own violent snore – punctures the skin of his sleep and he rises to the surface, slow-witted, stupid, his mind and limbs thick.

Then he remembers, and says 'No,' out loud, as if that will make a difference.

He goes to the kitchen and opens a beer. He decides to make cabbage rolls, from his mother's old recipe. They take time, but they're worth it.

He boils the cabbage, then spreads the leaves on a board. He seasons the ground beef, adds minced onion and grated potato, and folds the cabbage leaves into careful envelopes around the meat mixture.

A lizard darts across the white wall, then stops. Yellow-tailed, unblinking. All knees and elbows. 'I see you,' the old man says.

He sautés diced onion and shredded cabbage in a large saucepan, puts the rolls on top, adds prunes and a little water, and lets it simmer for a while.

He looks out the window. He can no longer imagine the future.

He carefully transfers the cabbage rolls to a casserole dish, squeezes lemon juice and drizzles syrup over them, then covers them with sliced tomatoes. He covers the dish, puts it in the oven. They need a couple of hours of slow heat.

He will write a letter to his great-niece. He finds writing paper and a pen, opens another beer, and goes out to the veranda.

He writes, *Your sister-in-law Sara left for the airport a little while ago. We had a nice dinner last night, and a good swim today. I gave her some advice that should boost her confidence. She needed some pointers on grooming, and attitude, from a man's point of view. I think she feels better now.*

The sun is going down. The old man sips his beer and wonders if he has ever understood much of anything. He thinks of how Larissa Lawson's beautiful arms arced droplets of water across the bay, and how the world is tilted towards loss, the way it once tilted towards love.

I had a beautiful young woman in my house last night, he writes. He thinks of her tight-shut mouth in that pale face, nipples brushing the flimsy fabric. Pressing so hard the nib almost gouges the paper, he adds, *Did you think I was no longer capable of getting an erection?*

The old man closes his eyes. The cabbage rolls take time, but they're worth every minute. He sits there, on the veranda, thinking he should probably baste them, but he doesn't move. He sits there while it gets dark, and the tree frogs and crickets start up their racket.

LORNA GETS A TATTOO

Lorna had no intention of getting a tattoo. She'd gone out for a decaf latte, and half an hour later she was in a tattoo parlour on Queen West, letting a burly goateed guy named Al – who looked as if most of the exposed areas of his skin had been spray-painted in lurid Technicolor by someone experiencing extremely disturbing hallucinations involving snakes, tongues, eyeballs and fire – ink a discreet flaming sun on the left side of her abdomen, about an inch below her navel.

'That's in*sane*,' her daughter Jess, a psych major, said when Lorna called her that evening. 'Tattoos look ridiculous on wrinkled skin.'

Zane, her son, raised his eyebrows when she showed him the tattoo. 'Cool,' he nodded, then reverted to looking dully at some point below and beyond her eyes for a few moments before he slunk back to his room and Marilyn Manson.

'Oh God,' her friend Kathy exclaimed into the phone. 'What were you *think*ing? I hope he used clean needles. And dye – there must be a backwash. You didn't get a red one, did you? Red dyes can give you really bad allergic reactions, even years later.'

After Lorna hung up the phone, she wondered what kind of allergic reactions. Hives? Chronic fatigue? Anaphylactic shock? Total immune system shutdown? Her sun was entirely blue, but a few years down the road they'd probably say *Oops, sorry – the blue ones cause excruciatingly painful stuff you don't even want to contemplate.*

No way would she ever tell her mother. There was something almost pornographic about it: *Lorna Gets a Tattoo.* Sort of like *Debbie Does Dallas.*

She peeked at the scab forming under the dressing on her belly and felt thrilled, as if she'd blown most of a paycheque on outrageous lingerie.

For the past month or so, Lorna had been in a state of semi-permanent stagefright-type fear, with sudden inexplicable attacks of out-of-the-blue terror so intense that her roiling stomach would lurch into sickening cartwheels and her heart thumped and slammed against the walls of her chest as if a small animal were trapped in there.

'Must be the start of menopause,' her friend Kathy had said, somewhat smugly.

'You're probably a little anemic, dear,' her mother, who attributed all kinds of ailments to anemia, had told her.

When Lorna was a child, some nights she'd lie awake while her bed began to tilt and spin serenely, and the walls of her room distorted like stretched putty. She'd hear her thrumming heartbeat, the blood surging past her ears, the hissing radiators, the buzz of stale air, the drone of the television in her parents' room – all these sounds dulled and warbled together into a deep, slow, warped resonance that vibrated from the skewed corners of her bedroom. It was as if the sound had burbled up from some vast menacing darkness at the centre of the universe; or worse – as if it came from inside *her*; from something horrible, oozing, monstrous.

Her mother had attributed those episodes to anemia too, and made little Lorna ingest daily doses of a vile-tasting tonic. Lorna learned to be more careful about what information she shared with her mother.

A week before the tattoo, Lorna had an appointment with a therapist recommended by the receptionist at the PR company where she worked. The therapist had an earnest, slightly strained expression that Lorna decided must have resulted from the effort of projecting Extreme Sensitivity, but which had the unfortunate effect of making her appear to suffer from acute gastric distress.

Lorna described the anxiety attacks. The therapist frowned, then handed her a clipboard with a few sheets of paper and a pen, and suggested that Lorna's Inner Child write Lorna a letter.

She must be joking, Lorna thought – *this is such a cliché*. She gave a half-giggle. 'Shouldn't I be embracing my Inner Crone instead?'

The therapist blinked, smiled benignly.

Fear prickled at Lorna's neck. 'I can't do this.'

'Sure you can.' The therapist's voice reminded Lorna of curdled milk. She smiled encouragement, oozed empathy. 'Are you right-handed? Use your left hand.'

Lorna blushed as she picked up the pen. Her palms were sweaty. She put the pen down. 'My Inner Child has absolutely nothing to say.'

'Of course she does.' She was soothing but brisk, like a plastic-gloved dental hygienist urging Lorna to open wider. 'You're being overwhelmed by unresolved fears you've ignored for years. Let her tell you what she needs.'

Oh, what the hell. Lorna picked up the pen again. 'Dear Lorna,' she wrote. The handwriting was almost illegible. She had very little control over her left hand. 'I want to sit by a warm fire with some hot tea and lots of books and the Dvorjak Violin Concerto playing. Love, Me.'

A crock, but it would do. She handed the therapist the clipboard.

'That's lovely,' the therapist cooed, the words dropping like blobs of yogurt. She nodded. Tapped tapered opalescent fingernails on the letter. She looked up at Lorna. Her eyes were blue-and-white smoke. The thin mouth twisted into an apologetic smile. 'But you've misspelled Dvořák.'

Before Lorna left, the therapist gave her a mirror. 'I want you to look at yourself and say, "Lorna, I love you just as you are. I accept you totally. You are safe. You are protected. You are adored."' She spoke with the exaggerated enunciation of someone giving directions to a person who has a limited understanding of English.

Lorna looked in the mirror. Her mouth was hanging open. She shut it. Something weird was happening with the passage of time, as if the cosmic batteries were running low. Protracted nanoseconds unwound and hung suspended while a relentlessly slow drone vibrated across her skull. She could barely breathe. She stood up and carefully put the mirror face-up on the therapist's desk.

'Sorry,' she whispered. Heart bashing, blood singing, she walked out.

She ran the five blocks to the subway. As she stood panting on the platform, she decided that instead of an Inner Child, she was harbouring a grotesque and slimy incubus. The sounds it uttered vibrated on wavelengths far beyond physical sound, and they merged with the vibrations of her thoughts. Occasionally her incubus slithered out and slapped a hideously deformed hand on her ankle, or draped itself around her waist and she'd have to kick free before it dragged her into an unimaginable darkness.

'I've tried everything,' Lorna had said to Graham, her ex-husband, at a restaurant a few nights after her visit to the therapist. 'Tranquillizers. Tequila. Massages. Disgusting herbal concoctions that stink up the entire house. Rescue Remedy. Qi-gong. Dope. I even tried acupuncture, twice: I lay there for half an hour with a bunch of needles stuck in my head and stomach. I'm spending a fortune and nothing helps.'

She and Graham had promised to behave decently to one another when they'd separated, four years ago. They made a point of meeting at least once a month.

'So what's going on? Why the panic?'

'I wish I knew. Nothing in particular. All kinds of things, I suppose. Tornadoes. Lethal viruses. Pesticides. Flesh-eating bacteria. I'm afraid something terrible will happen to one of the kids, or the dog will develop some sort of weird tumour and die. I'm afraid one day I'll no longer have the will to get out of bed in the morning. I'm scared of losing my grip and falling right off this planet. Do you have any idea how fast it's going?'

Graham closed his eyes. 'Jesus, Lorna.'

'Sixty-six thousand six hundred miles an hour. More or less. Unbelievably quickly.'

He reached for her trembling hands across the table. His grip was firm and warm. She'd almost forgotten the nights he'd snored steadily beside her and she'd wanted to cradle him against her breast but instead she just lay there in the dark, rigid.

'Maybe you need a lover.'

'Oh, give me a break. I tell you I'm getting these off-the-Richter-scale panic attacks, and your brilliant solution is, Wow, she really needs to get laid. That's just typical.'

There had been no infidelities in their marriage, no major arguments over aging in-laws. Just a gradual divergence and the slow evaporation of love.

'Come on, don't get so defensive. That's not what I meant.'

Graham had dated a twenty-four-year-old stripper for a couple of months last year. He'd been too embarrassed to introduce her to any of his friends. He'd once confessed, soon after he and Lorna separated, that he was afraid of growing old alone.

'Anyway,' she said, 'sex has become too dangerous.'

'Lighten up, Lorna. Go on vacation. Pamper yourself. Do something reckless.'

Lorna sighed. Her idea of living dangerously was to stop in a no-park zone while she dashed into the store for milk. 'It's like when you're a kid and you've checked under the bed three times already and you've made your parents check too, but no matter how stupid you know it is, the second you turn out the light you're absolutely sure there's something really scary under there.'

She picked up her drink. Her heart had gone berserk, palpitating in wildly arrhythmic riffs. She attempted a nonchalant smile, but her hands shook so much the glass clinked painfully against her teeth. Red wine splashed on the tablecloth and stained the sleeve of her blouse.

Graham slowly shook his head.

Lorna knocked on Zane's bedroom door when she returned home from dinner with Graham. Zane lay on his bed with the volume on his stereo turned up so high she could feel the bass vibrating in her jaw. She worried about whether he might have permanent hearing damage. He responded to her shouted questions in monosyllables. No, he wasn't hungry. Yes, he was fine. No one called for her. Yes, he'd walked the dog. Would she shut the door on her way out.

She made some tranquillizing valerian tea, lit one of those aromatherapy candles that promise sedation, and took a long, warm bath. Afterwards, she sat in bed with the dog stretched out at her knees, and wrote a list:

Things I am afraid of
- Unnamed groping things that lurk under beds
- Slow distorted voices that drone in stretching night rooms
- Tidal waves
- Falling away from the world

When she turned out the light, Lorna reflected that of course, in a way, Graham was right. The therapist too, with her earnestly proffered mirror. Lorna knew – everybody knows – that to be loved, to give love, is what we all need.

And then, on the verge of sleep, there it was, projecting itself on her squeezed-shut eyelids. Twisting and leering, it shrank and expanded, looming at the rim of her consciousness, changing form and position quicker than a housefly on amphetamines.

She opened her eyes and groped for the dog. How the hell do you get rid of an incubus? Colonic irrigation would be useless; a juice fast or bulimic purge wouldn't do a damn thing.

The dog moved away from her grasp and settled at her feet with a sigh. Lorna longed to hold someone. This urge to embrace came upon her at odd moments. She'd be talking to a client or sitting at the movies or in a waiting room, and suddenly she'd have to resist a desperate need to lean over and wrap her arms around the person beside her.

When she finally closed her eyes again, the incubus was gone.

The following evening, Lorna made dinner for herself and Zane – a well-balanced meal with plenty of fresh vegetables – even though she didn't feel like cooking. She washed the dishes and wiped the counters. She walked the dog around the block – she'd asked Zane to do it, but he said wait until he'd finished recording something. Then she called her mother to ask how she was, knowing her mother would keep her on the phone too long. By the time she was able to hang up, she'd missed the first ten minutes of the movie she wanted to watch on TV, so she had a bath instead. It occurred to Lorna as she lay in the bathtub that she generally behaved well, even when she didn't feel like it. She never threw tantrums; she scooped up after the dog even if nobody was looking; she bathed regularly. She made allowances for surly teenagers who could be ungrateful and sometimes cruel. She tried not to insult people. She returned phone calls, sent thank-you notes for gifts, and Christmas cards to people she didn't give a damn about. She greeted neighbours politely, even when they'd sprayed their lawns with pesticide. But this thing inside her – this wild, monstrous, twisting thing – it was the won't-behave, the deliberately careless, the downright nasty, the rotten-to-the-core. It smirked and undermined and sabotaged. It knew how to short-circuit an orderly existence; it knew what hissed seductions could spoil a settled life and turn it rancid.

Half an hour before Lorna drifted into the tattoo parlour, she sat sipping her decaf latte, thinking half her life was over, and when had she become so afraid? One long-ago sunny afternoon – she was probably even younger than her daughter Jess was now – she'd stood on the back deck of a communal house, naked except for a pair of bikini panties, while her friends painted her body and Blind Faith blared through the open door. Zenon, an art student, used one of her nipples as the centre of a daisy; Stephanie painted a rainbow across her belly; Nick swirled abstract designs along her thighs.

She wiped biscotti crumbs from her mouth and sipped her latte. Back then she'd been sunstruck, lovestruck, lifestruck. She longed for those days when she could stand on a rickety deck and allow friends to smear paint on her skin with warm fingers, to daub her with soaked brushes while she stood with arms extended, mouth slack with delight, poised like a beautiful diver in the blaze of the sun.

Lorna is chopping onions for pasta sauce when the phone rings. It's Graham, wanting to know if she'll see a play with him tomorrow night.

'Sorry,' she says, 'I'm busy tomorrow.'

He asks if she's okay, and says Jess told him about the tattoo. What made her do a thing like that?

'Ah, well, you've got to love your Inner Incubus.'

'Your what?'

'Nothing. Just kidding.'

She washes parsley, slices mushrooms, crushes garlic. She is listening to music while she prepares the meal – a compilation tape Jess made her for Mother's Day. She's had the tattoo for five days now. It's like getting a great new haircut or a gorgeous silk dress – she'll be striding down the street, arms swinging, and she feels she could smash right through the sidewalk. She sometimes has an almost irresistible urge to run her fingertips over her tattoo. She'll unbutton jeans or slip a hand down the waistband of a skirt and, with her eyes closed, she tries to locate it, as if subtle differences in temperature or texture distinguish it from the surrounding skin. She thinks of Al, the tattoo artist, who had bent over her, working mostly in silence, his huge tattooed hands surprisingly adept and gentle. She'd been moved by his intense, almost tender, concentration.

An Ani DiFranco song on Jess's tape yanks at Lorna, spins her around. She puts down the knife and dances with a sudden explosion of joy. Zane walks into the kitchen and finds his mother whirling and stomping and swaying.

'I'm hungry,' he says.

When she doesn't respond, just keeps on dancing, he opens the fridge and grabs a slice of leftover pizza.

Lorna moves towards him, corners him, dances around him. She holds out her arms. 'Come. Dance with me.'

Zane shakes his head and hunches sideways over his pizza as if to protect it from her. He dodges past her, gives her a you're-definitely-certifiable look as he leaves, but he's grinning.

Lorna dances to the kitchen door, opens it, and dances out, onto the deck. Music pulses through her as she spins in the dark. The wind is on her upturned throat and she wants to leap right up and swipe the gleaming moon.

SMILE ON MRS G

It is Sunday afternoon, and Mrs G has been invited over, on her way to visit her husband in the hospital. Mr G will be dead within two weeks, of cancer.

Mother has baked scones (Oh no, not those again, Father says, but she shrugs, Oh well, too bad, don't eat them then) and put out whipped cream, and raspberry jam in the cut-glass bowl with the tiny silver spoon. The coffee table is set: crocheted doily on the teak tray; quilted cosy on the teapot; the best cups and saucers, inspected first for chips or fine cracks; tannin stains have been quickly scoured off with baking soda.

Mrs G doesn't notice that Mother has gone to so much trouble. She sits hunched and thin and sallow in the slipcovered armchair, antimacassar askew behind her lank mousy hair, and twists the edges of her napkin in her lap. Her scone sits half-eaten on the small table at her side. Father refused one when offered, pulling a face that Mother ignored, but the Child has had two, smothered in cream, and raises her eyebrows, pleading, at Mother – another one, please? Mother shakes her head and gives a quick frown, then asks Mrs G, More tea? But Mrs G still has half a cup, so Mother asks about Mrs G's son and daughter, and Mrs G's in-laws who live, squabbling and disapproving and generally bedridden, with the Gs. Father tamps his pipe and lights it. Mrs G blinks as she speaks, as if to get a clearer picture, to make sense of things, and cocks her head like a budgie. She has a thin, whining voice. Father leans back in his chair and clears his throat and bites on the pipe stem. He would much rather be reading, or listening to the radio. The Child is bored too and is about to excuse herself when Mrs G begins to cry. She cries quietly – just one muffled sob and then a shuddering, silent weeping, her hands wringing and twisting the napkin in her lap.

Father shifts and frowns and taps at his pipe and tries to catch Mother's eye – do something, can't you? but Mother doesn't look at him, she looks at Mrs G and bites her lower lip and lifts her hand and opens her mouth as if to say something, then she draws in air and lets her hand drop down. Mrs G has taken a folded tissue from the sleeve of her cardigan and she wipes her eyes and nose but she goes on crying and wringing, wringing, and the Child is alarmed, horrified because adults are not supposed to cry although it is different with Mrs G because she must be so sad, so terribly sad (Poor fellow, he's not long for this world, Father had said before Mrs G arrived). The Child thinks she should probably leave the room, tiptoe away but she doesn't want to draw attention to herself, it wouldn't be polite, she should pretend she hasn't noticed that Mrs G is crying, and then Mother goes over to Mrs G and puts her hand on her shoulder. She hands her another tissue, and Mrs G blows her nose and sniffs, I'm sorry, I'm sorry.

Mother says, soft and gentle, Don't be sorry, it's good to cry, dear, go on and let it all out, and she waits until Mrs G's crying stops.

Now, Mother says in a different, stricter voice, You've been neglecting yourself. When last did you have your hair done?

Mrs G peers up at Mother and blinks. She blinks and frowns and looks as if she is about to burst into tears again, then gives her head a shake. I don't know, she says, and lifts a tentative hand to her hair, I can't remember.

Fine, Mother says, brisk and cheerful, We're going to do your hair. It'll make you feel better. You mustn't let yourself go, it's not doing him any good to see you like this. Come – and Mrs G stands, slowly looking around as if she has wandered into the wrong place and is trying to find the way out, and allows herself to be ushered to the bathroom. Mother calls to the Child, Please bring a clean towel from the linen chest.

Mrs G is bending forward over the basin. She has a frayed pink towel draped over her narrow shoulders, and holds a washcloth over her face to stop the shampoo from getting into her eyes. Mother's fingers are massaging, rubbing Mrs G's scalp, lathering the shampoo vigorously as if to scrub away the mousiness, as if to wash away layers of

dulling grime so that real, vivid colours can show through. Mrs G's
ears jut out from the sides of her head, their tips pointy and pink as
she raises her head so that Mother can empty the soapy basin and
refill it with clean water. The little hollow that is formed at the nape
of Mrs G's neck is sad and thin and trembly, and the Child stands at
the open bathroom door and watches the hollow, watches it bob
slightly with the pressure of Mother's fingers. Mother sometimes
washes the Child's hair in the basin, massaging gently and rinsing
with clear warm water, filling a bucket or a pitcher with the rinsing
water and pouring slowly so that a tickle forms at the back of the
Child's throat. Then she wraps a clean towel around the Child's head
and the Child smiles at herself, turbaned in the mirror, an exotic
princess with a damp tendril snaking from the towel and rainbow
droplets of water on glistening eyelashes. She remembers being
bathed in the basin once, long long ago, her whole naked body
squeezed in, slimy soap slipping over her, giggling, giggling, knees
close to her chin (Careful, Mother said, Mind the taps – you won't be
able to fit in here much longer).

Wait a minute, we're not done yet; three rinses, Mother says.

Oh, Mrs G says, in her voice that is always saying sorry, sorry for
having a voice – I only do two.

No dear, you need three rinses. You should do three rinses when
you wash clothes too, for that matter. You're not getting all the soap
out of your hair with two, that's why you're getting dandruff.

I never knew, says Mrs G, and her voice trails off, sorry, sorry for
the dandruff, sorry for the nuisance, and Mother wants to grab her
pathetic shoulders and shake, to heave some life into her, or to hug
her damp head fiercely and say, There, there, while her throat aches
for this poor, wretched woman.

Mother rinses gently, and moves the towel from the sloped
shoulders and wraps it around the ears, around the dripping rope of
hair, twists it into a turban, There, all done. The sunlight slants in,
beams in through the window and catches Mrs G on the cheek,
across her left eye, but she doesn't look anything like an exotic
princess, and she blinks, blinks, as she sees herself in the mirror, the

network of fine veins branching out from the sides of her nose, spreading over her shiny washed face.

Mother rubs Mrs G's head briskly with the towel, and runs a comb through her hair. Mrs G watches in the mirror and her eyes fill with tears because her hair is being pulled. She blinks harder with the tears and Mother says, Am I hurting? Oh no, no, Mrs G replies, and blinks, blinks, her head tugged with each pull of the comb.

The sunlight that streams in through the window and shines onto the side of Mrs G's face makes her shake her head ever-so-slightly, as if there were a buzzing, the breeze of insect wings, and the Child, seeing the white tiles around the mirror, remembers the cold tiles of the bathroom floor when Mrs G's daughter slept over, ages ago, and they locked themselves in the bathroom. Mrs G's daughter got to be the doctor because she was almost three years older and the Child had to be the patient, and the daughter with her dirty yellow hair and fat-cheeked face like a yellow apple made the Child lie down and remove her panties; she said, You have to, that's what doctors do, they even stick their fingers up, they wear plastic gloves – and the Child, not sure she believed but now even more afraid of doctors asked Mother the next day after Mrs G's daughter had gone home if it was true and Mother said, Where on earth did you hear such nonsense? and the Child told, quietly, because Mother was so cross and the Child wasn't supposed to tell tales or say rude things. We'll have to keep you away from that girl, Mother had said, and the Child was glad, because something about that girl's skinned, scabby knees, something about her dirty yellow hair, something about her sly smile that pushed out the yellow apple cheeks made the Child feel itchy, as if worms were crawling over her, and maybe she wouldn't have to go to the Gs' house any more where the drapes are heavy and dark and the smudgy windows let suffocating yellow light drift over dust mites, over dark wood, over high beds with dark heavy headboards and footboards and dark heavy bedspreads and grandparents who live in the house, in the beds, with trays of half-eaten food next to them, complaining and calling for Mrs G who shuffles in, shoulders bent forward, knees never straightening, who whispers through the house and whines at her children, her head bobbing like a car ornament, her eyes blinking, blinking, at the sad mustiness of it all.

Come, dear, Mother says, and leads Mrs G to her bedroom, where she seats her at the stool in front of the vanity and takes out a tin full of bobby pins. The Child tiptoes in, slips up onto the bed and watches, dangling her legs over the side. Mother takes strands of hair and deftly winds them around her index finger, twisting them into spirals that she secures with bobby pins. She does her own hair like this at night, sleeps in pin curls with an old pair of panties clipped over her head to keep the curls from loosening. When she has finished curling Mrs G's hair she plugs in the hair dryer with its flexible tube and the tie-on plastic cap that balloons out as the warm air blows into it. She gives Mrs G a magazine and goes downstairs to clean up the tea things, and to see if Father, who is happily listening to the radio, needs anything (Just a kiss). The Child goes off to draw pictures of people, making them beautiful with her eraser and coloured pencils.

Mrs G sits with the magazine open in her lap, but she is not reading. She is thinking of Mr G, who looks like a shrivelled old man now, hollow and bony and fading; she thinks of his hands that flap like trapped butterflies with the pain and she is surprised to find herself wondering when last those hands flitted across her body; she thinks of the doctors who shake their heads gloomily: hopeless, hopeless; she thinks of Mr G's parents who complain and accuse, as if even this is her fault, this illness that is erasing their son.

She is startled when Mother comes to test a curl, to see if it has dried. I must have dozed off, she says (sorry, sorry).

Mother removes the bobby pins and combs Mrs G's hair into soft curls, standing behind her and fluffing the hair around her ears. She calls to the Child – Be a dear and bring my lipstick; it's in my purse. The Child runs off to get the pretty gold case with the lipstick that appears at the end of the swivel tube like a bright red crayon. Mother is applying rouge (Just a little, a bit of colour) to Mrs G's pallid cheeks, frowning with concentration, then stepping back to assess the results. She dabs blue eye shadow on Mrs G's eyelids, then wipes the end of the lipstick with a tissue. Mrs G looks bewildered, looks as if she might cry again, but now there is blue when she blinks.

The Child is disappointed. Mother has not managed to make Mrs G beautiful. She still looks like Mrs G, only now she has clean curly hair and pink cheeks and blue-rimmed eyes.

The Child feels a longing ballooning in her, so strong it makes her squirm and hop: she wants to paint the lipstick on Mrs G's mouth. Please Mommy can I put it on oh please let me, she whispers, and Mother replies, Well, I'm not sure – then Mrs G blinks (blue) and gives the Child a quick tight smile, and says, Yes, of course, go on, put it on, and the Child takes it and reaches out her hand, clutching the lipstick like a crayon. She is going to colour Mrs G.

But it is hopeless. Mrs G will never look anything but nervous and tired and defeated; Mr G will still have cancer (and who knows what the doctors will do to him, poking at him with their plastic-gloved fingers); the daughter and her big brother will still be sly and covered in scabs; and the Child is suddenly angry, a hot flush of fury rises up into her cheeks. And she will reach out and scribble, she will smear a clown mouth, a hideous grin, a huge smudge of blood across the tight thin lips. Then before they can stop her, because they are so shocked, she is so quick, she will rub the lipstick across the cheeks, making uneven red blotches, harlequin circles, she will draw blood red across Mrs G's sad face until tears prick Mrs G's eyes and Mrs G screams and screams and screams.

She reaches out her hand, lipstick clutched like a crayon, and moves it slowly towards Mrs G's pursed mouth and Mrs G blinks, her eyes smiling, kind and gentle. Carefully, carefully, the Child applies the lipstick, managing to do it without a single smudge, managing to stay exactly within the lines. Then Mrs G draws herself up, straight, she breathes in deeply and pushes back her shoulders. She turns her head, slowly, from side to side. Her hands flutter, her fingers dart up like sparrows and pat her new curls as she studies her reflection in the mirror, and a giggle escapes her perfect red mouth.

ORPHANS ARE LIKE THIS

Jailhouse phones way too early on a Saturday morning, saying, 'It's me, sorry, did I wake you?' She tells Claudia that Iris has taken a turn for the worse.

'Ah, jeez,' Claudia breathes and sinks back into the pillow. She's thinking, *It's okay, it's not Trish,* while post-panic toxins sluice through every cell of her body. She opens her eyes and squints at the clock radio: 7:10. 'I'll be there,' she promises, her tongue ungluing itself from the roof of her mouth, 'soon as I get organized.'

Jailhouse says, 'Okaybyebye,' the way she always does, quick and high, the syllables toppling into one another like a little stampede.

Before Claudia heads over to the bus depot she leaves messages for Trish at six different places, asking her to get down to Iris's, ASAP. If she's more specific, she figures Trish won't show. As it is, chances are slim her sister will actually get any of the messages.

These days Trish mostly lives in her beat-up Toyota hatchback with Henry, her dog. She surfaces at Claudia's apartment from time to time when she wants a loan or a hot bath. Sometimes she and Henry camp out on Claudia's pullout sofa for days or weeks on end and watch TV. Henry, an occasionally incontinent ninety-pound wolfhound-collie mix, sighs at the screen and chews on rawhide strips and slobbers all over the cushions while Trish spills ash and ketchup and red wine and litters the carpet with candy wrappers. By the time they leave, the place looks like a crime scene.

It's been at least a couple of months since Claudia last saw her sister. For all she knows, Trish could have driven west or south until she found a decent beach someplace warm. Driving makes Trish happy.

Claudia sometimes thinks she and Trish might as well be joined at the hip, dragging one another around like reluctant Siamese twins. She believes most orphans are like this. The two of them have been orphans ever since their father blew himself up one Sunday afternoon when Claudia was fourteen and Trish twelve. He accidentally detonated a small bomb – a rusted souvenir of World War II – that the previous owners of their house had inexplicably left on a shelf in the garage alongside half-filled cans of motor oil and paint thinner. He'd been married to Iris for just over a year when this happened, and Claudia and Trish's own mother had already been dead long enough to become almost perfect.

Claudia is standing outside her old house in a dismal November drizzle and pressing the door buzzer. Iris has never bothered repairing the bomb-damaged garage, other than nailing flimsy pieces of plywood over the more obvious holes. Claudia thinks bitterly that this is what they have all done to varying degrees during the eighteen years since her father blew himself to bits: slapped unsatisfactory patches over gaping chasms and left it at that.

Jailhouse finally opens the door. 'Oh,' she says. 'It's you.'

'Who the hell did you expect?' Claudia snaps. Jailhouse would probably piss off Pollyanna, even without the drizzle and sleep-deprivation. Trish was the one who first called her Jailhouse. Claudia can't remember why exactly – maybe because she's always been lanky and shapeless as an iron bar; maybe because she so seldom leaves the house; maybe because being forced to hang out with her is like serving a long stretch of hard time. Her real name is Marlene.

'Uh,' Jailhouse says, scratching the top of her head and looking as if all the wind has been knocked out of her, 'nobody really. Sorry.'

Claudia feels a spasm of remorse. She puts her bag down on the floor, brushes droplets of water off her hair and leather jacket and gives Jailhouse a limp hug. It's like hugging a slug – her stepsister barely responds. Claudia squeezes Jailhouse's stooped shoulders. She resists the temptation to shake her, stands back and says, 'You look exhausted. Did you get any sleep?'

Jailhouse appears to consider this for a moment before replying. 'I don't think so.'

'How's she doing?'

'Not good. She's basically not even getting out of bed any more. Right now I think she's sleeping.'

'Shouldn't she be in hospital?'

'She won't go.' Jailhouse glances up at the stairs and stage-whispers, 'She says she wants to die at home.'

'Hoo boy.' Claudia's cheeks balloon as she exhales through her teeth. 'Well,' she whispers back, 'I guess we have to respect that.'

Jailhouse nods slowly.

'I left a bunch of messages for Trish,' Claudia tells her. 'She might be coming as well.'

'Oh? That'll be nice,' Jailhouse says unconvincingly.

'Although you never know with Trish.'

'No.'

After a minute or two, Claudia says, 'Go get some rest. I'll take over. But I could really use a coffee.'

Jailhouse looks at her blankly, then opens her eyes wide. 'Sorry. I should have offered. I wasn't thinking.'

Iris's rheumy eyes, when they eventually open, look as if most of the colour has been boiled out of them. Iris wheezes as she fixes them on Claudia. 'Where's Marlene?' is all she manages to gasp before convulsing into a gagging coughing fit.

'Iris?' Claudia says when the coughing subsides. 'Hi! It's me, Claudia.'

Iris hawks and dabs at the pinkish spittle in the corner of her mouth. 'I see that,' she says faintly. 'What's wrong?'

'Nothing's wrong,' Claudia says. She reaches over from the bedside chair and pats Iris's hand. The skin feels clammy and thin as rice paper. 'I came to see you. You're not feeling so good?'

Iris opens her mouth, takes a few laboured breaths and starts to cough again. Her chest heaves and shudders and she makes alarming choking noises. 'I'm dying,' she whispers when she stops coughing. 'What happened to Marlene?'

'She's here. She's just having a little rest. Can I get you anything? Something to drink maybe?'

Iris rolls her head weakly to and fro on the pile of pillows and flaps her hand in the air as if she would like to swat Claudia clear out of the room. This precipitates another episode of coughing. Jailhouse appears in the doorway, her face pinched with worry. 'Is she okay? Mom? Are you okay?'

'Relax, everything's under control,' Claudia says. 'Did you manage to sleep?'

'Look,' Iris tells Jailhouse. 'Claudia's here.' She pauses for a moment to catch her breath. 'What do you think of that?'

On that long-ago Sunday, while police and ambulance workers swarmed around the garage, Iris refused to let Claudia and Trish outside. With her arms flung out sideways, she stood blocking the front door. 'Go back upstairs,' she told them, her face contorting wildly. Jailhouse was cowering slack-mouthed beside her.

'Why? What's going on?' Claudia asked. The stereo in their bedroom had been blaring so loudly that the floorboards shook and they had taken some time to realize something was amiss.

'Just go!' Iris shouted.

Trish's lower lip trembled. 'Where's our dad?'

'What happened? Why can't we see him?'

'Because I said so. Now get back upstairs, this minute!'

'Where is he?' Claudia demanded.

'Dad!'

'Why can't we see him?'

Finally Iris blurted out, 'Because he's dead, for Chrissakes.'

Just like that. And then Trish kicked Iris hard on the shin, ducked under her collapsing arm and bolted.

It's late afternoon and still raining when the doorbell rings. All the way from the kitchen, where Claudia is making soup, she can hear Henry bark.

She opens the door and Henry's entire body squirms with joy. Trish is right beside him, grinning. 'Shitty weather,' Trish says as Henry yelps and leaps up, thumping massive muddy paws against

Claudia's chest and almost bowling her over. 'Whoa Henry!' Claudia gasps. 'Hey boy, down. Hi, Trish. You came.' She massages Henry's ears and neck until his hind leg begins to jerk up and down. He gives himself a vigorous shake and sneezes so hard his nose whacks the floor, then he swipes Claudia's legs with his wagging tail as he brushes past her and bounds off towards the kitchen.

'I'm intrigued,' Trish says as she totters in. She has on a wet pair of knee-high snakeskin boots with three-inch spike heels. She obviously has no intention of removing them. 'So. What's up?' She fumbles with the buttons on her oversized jacket, shrugs it off and flings it over the banister. Claudia's jaw drops. Above a pair of ripped black hipster leggings her sister is wearing a stained midriff-exposing T-shirt that says DRUNK 24:7 and apparently it's not lying. Trish is tanked, or at least half-tanked. She is also very pregnant.

'Jesus, Trish,' Claudia says. 'Why didn't you tell me?'

'I was waiting for the perfect moment, darling,' Trish purrs. 'Champagne, candlelight. Men with guitars. This weather really *sucks.*' She plants a sloppy kiss on Claudia's still-open mouth.

'Wow.' Claudia feels so light-headed she braces herself against the wall. 'You look like you swallowed a whole watermelon.'

'Really? Because I never get to look in a mirror. Lemme see.' Trish has always been skinny as a scribble, skinny as barbed wire. She wobbles over to the hall closet and examines herself in the full-length mirror inside its door. 'Hah!' she says, turning this way and that and patting her protruding bare belly.

'Whose baby is it?'

'What do you mean, whose baby? Dumb question. It's mine.'

'You know what I mean. Who's the father?'

Trish waves her arm in a gesture of dismissal. 'Nobody. The father's totally irrelevant. He's history. So why am I here?'

'What?'

'You called. I was summoned. What's going on?'

'Iris is really sick,' Claudia says.

'Yeah? What's wrong?'

'Heart failure. She's had it a while already. It's pretty bad.'

'Heart failure?' Trish gives a derisive snort. 'Jesus! Who's surprised?'

'She's dying, Trish. Have a little respect.'

'Pffft!'

When Trish was a college student she ran the highly successful campus radio station. During her final semester she wrote to the president of a major recording company, asking for a job. To everyone's surprise he hired her – initially in accounts, later in P.R. Eventually she was given the task of chaperoning a semi-famous rock star whose substance abuse is legendary. Trish was supposed to get her to interviews and performances on time, clean and sober. Trish and the rock star got along like a house on fire, with the upshot that Trish's subsequent fondness for illicit substances rivalled that of the rock star. But still, Claudia thinks, looking at her sister, everything about her current state – her filthy uncombed hair, her clothes, her inebriation, even her pregnancy – seems calculated to piss off Iris.

'Hello,' Jailhouse says, coming down the stairs.

'Jailhouse.' Trish places a hand over her heart and adopts an expression of extreme faux concern. 'I am *so sorry.*'

'Thank you, Trish.' Jailhouse's gaze fixes on Trish's bulging belly. She frowns and gives her head a little shake. 'Um, she's awake if you want to come up. Well, he*llo.*' Her voice suddenly rises by an octave or two as Henry races towards her. She is one of those people who sound as if they have gulped substantial amounts of helium whenever they talk to animals or small children. 'Hello, doggie, hello. Oops!' she says as Henry buries his snout in her crotch. 'Okay boy. Okay, that's enough.'

Henry pounds up the stairs ahead of them and races into Iris's bedroom, thwacking the dresser with his tail. Trish staggers in behind him, blowing exaggerated air-kisses in the direction of Iris's bed.

Iris grimaces. 'She brought that damn dog?' she wheezes.

'Henry, out!' Claudia says, pointing at the door.

'Happy to see you too. My God,' Trish says, turning to Claudia, 'you're right. She really looks terrible. Her colour is *shocking.*' Trish eases herself onto the bedside chair. 'So,' she says to Iris. 'Isn't this fun? A family reunion?'

Iris stares at her, stone-faced.

The last time Trish came, for an ill-advised Christmas a couple of years ago shortly before she headed off to rehab, they were all sitting around the table for dinner. While Iris carved the turkey, Trish removed the vial of cocaine she wore around her neck, dipped into it with the tiny spoon attached to its lid and took a generous snort of its contents. 'In my house? How dare you! It's *Christ*mas, for Chrissakes,' Iris had spluttered, the carving knife trembling in mid-air. And Trish had lifted her head, white powder coating the circumference of her left nostril. 'Oh, give me a break,' she said, and sniffed. 'That's precisely the point. Holidays depress me. I'm self-medicating.'

Iris glares at Trish a while then closes her eyes. 'Talking really tires her out,' Jailhouse whispers.

'Ah. So that explains it,' Trish says, taking out a cigarette.

'Oh, but you shouldn't smoke,' Jailhouse stammers.

'Are you kidding? Why not? I'll go outside if it bothers you. Rain and all.'

'Yes, but it's bad for the baby.'

The corners of Trish's mouth twitch as she studies Jailhouse's tremulous face. 'Thank you for that information, Jailhouse,' she says softly. 'I'll bear that in mind.'

When she leaves the room, Iris opens her eyes. 'That girl was always oversexed,' she says.

Claudia finds her sister at the open kitchen door, propped up against the jamb, her jacket slung over her shoulders. She's smoking and gazing out at the rain, which is now falling hard, whipped sideways by the wind. Most of the smoke is blowing back into the kitchen along with a stinging spray of rain.

'Trish?'

Trish doesn't even look at her. 'If you tell me she did the best she could for us, I'll puke.'

'It's freezing and there's rain coming in. Shut the door.'

'Fuck this.'

'Come on. Please shut the door?'

Trish sighs. She takes a couple of intense drags on her cigarette, flicks it into the yard and slams the door. 'I quit, you know. Everything. For six weeks I've been clean as a goddamn nun. Like not even one measly cigarette, and then I go off and buy a pack on the way over and it's almost half gone.'

'I shouldn't have asked you to come.'

'And a bottle of tequila. And I don't need one of your lectures.'

'I'm not saying anything.'

'You don't have to. I can see it all over your face.' Trish opens the fridge door and peers inside. Henry, miraculously awakened from a nap at the sound of the fridge opening, nudges up alongside her. Trish picks up a packet of bologna, sniffs it and wrinkles her nose. 'My God,' she says. 'This stuff should be quarantined. Why is there never anything to eat in this house?'

'I'm making soup.'

'Good. At least there's nothing in here with "Marlene" written on it.'

Claudia gives a hollow laugh. 'Seriously.' That was what Iris used to do – reserve choice items of food for Jailhouse, who was a ridiculously picky eater, by labelling them in ballpoint on torn-off strips of masking tape.

'How disgusting is that? That woman is the furthest thing from a decent human being.'

'Yeah, well. Iris is pretty clueless.'

Trish shakes her head. After a couple of minutes she says, 'That's it. I'm outta here.'

'Don't go. Stay for soup. It's horrible out there.'

Claudia isn't sure why she so desperately wants her sister here, *needs* her, but she will persuade her to stay, and later they will lie in their old twin beds with the lights out and talk softly, briefly, until they fall asleep. And in the sweet warmth of darkness, while Henry dream-twitches and snores on the rug between them, Claudia will scan the familiar shapes of the room, the shadowy bulk of her sister's body under the bedclothes, without the uncomfortable sense of intrusion she so often feels when she looks in Trish's eyes, that sense she is glimpsing things she should never have seen.

The following morning they decide to take Iris to hospital. It is actually Claudia who decides this – Jailhouse numbly agrees after a fretful night spent listening to her mother struggling to breathe. Trish doesn't care, and Iris is too ill to resist.

Jailhouse rides with Iris in the ambulance while Claudia and Trish follow in the Toyota. After some protest by both Henry and Trish, Henry is left behind in the house.

Trish's car is covered in stickers, inside and out – Day-Glo smiley faces and stars, Betty Boop and Minnie Mouse, cheesy slogans (*Somewhere an old lady is shouting 'Bingo!'*; *Mean people suck*; *Save the whales*) – and swamped with junk – batteries, empty cans, a moth-eaten blanket, a grungy sleeping bag, a beeswax candle in a rusty tin, Mars bars, piles of clothes, ground-up potato chips. A Wyclef tape is playing too loud and Trish is smoking incessantly while driving much too fast. They make a couple of wrong turns, and by the time they find parking and the right entrance to the hospital, Jailhouse is already signing forms at Admitting and Iris is hooked up to a daunting array of machines.

After a few hours of watching Iris and the beeping machines and questioning the nurses who breeze in and out to check vital signs, during which time Trish wanders off periodically and returns after lengthy intervals, Claudia suggests they all go for lunch. Not to the cafeteria, but out somewhere, for a walk, to clear their heads.

When they get out onto the street, Jailhouse pauses for a moment, shocked still by the sunlight. Then she begins to read the store and restaurant signs aloud as she walks – this is something she's done for as long as Claudia remembers – making them into barely audible stuttering ditties. 'Duh-duh-duh-*Dunkin' Donuts*,' she mumbles. 'Buh-buh-buh-buh-Beebee Bar*goons*.'

Trish jabs Claudia in the ribs. 'Is she for real?'

'The *Pick*le Barrel. Picklebarrelpicklebarrelpicklebarrel,' Jail-house repeats like a bizarre mantra. Sometimes she turns her attention to car licence plates. 'ABLN threefour*two*,' she hums.

'What?' Trish says.

'Huh?' Jailhouse frowns, apparently unaware she's doing it.

'Doesn't get out much, does she,' Trish mutters.

They pick up some wraps and coffee, which Claudia pays for, and afterwards make their way back to the hospital because Jailhouse is anxious about Iris. When they get there Iris is asleep, or else too weak or unwilling to open her eyes.

Trish fidgets in her chair and paces, fidgets and paces.

'Cut it out,' Claudia snaps.

Trish rolls her eyes, gives Claudia the finger, disappears for a while, reappears reeking of smoke. For a moment Claudia wonders if she's been drinking, then dismisses the thought. Trish examines the fluid dripping through the IV and the pulsing lines on the machines. 'Well, she's not flat-lining yet,' she announces, wiping her nose with the back of her hand. Claudia shoots her a warning look.

'I have to head back soon,' Claudia says eventually. 'I've got work tomorrow.'

'I'll drive you,' Trish says.

'We should take you home,' Claudia tells Jailhouse. 'You really need to sleep.'

Jailhouse hesitates.

'She'll be fine. They're watching her all the time.'

'Okay,' Jailhouse says.

'I'll be back next weekend,' Claudia promises as she bends over to kiss Iris's forehead.

Trish hoists herself out of the chair. She arches backwards, her hands on the small of her back, then grasps Iris's fingers, squeezing briefly. 'Bye,' she says. Iris's eyelids flutter half-open. She parts her lips with a popping sound as if she's blowing a small bubble, shuts her eyes and inhales.

Trish clears her throat and nods. 'Okay,' she says. 'Let's get this show on the road.'

'I'll drive,' Claudia says when they find the Toyota on the fourth floor of the parking garage.

'No way,' Trish says. 'You're a terrible driver.'

'Come on, Trish.' Claudia holds out her hand for the key. 'Let's just have an easy ride back, okay?'

Jailhouse slides onto the back seat. 'You're really starting to piss me off, you know that? Get in,' Trish tells Claudia.

Claudia shakes her head and goes over to the passenger side. Trish turns on the ignition, shifts the car into first and they lurch forward, narrowly missing a column. She slams on the brakes and grins at Claudia. 'Just kidding,' she says. She reverses, shifts back into first and accelerates the wrong way down a one-way aisle.

They race up a ramp, tires squealing. 'What the hell are you doing? The exit's the other way,' Claudia yells.

'Quick tour,' Trish says. She's driving like a kamikaze, zooming around the spiralling ramp until they reach the roof, then she screeches to a halt in a parking bay, winks at Claudia, whips the car around and tears back down the ramp to the exit.

'Jesus, Trish,' Claudia says when they're out on the street. 'Slow down!'

'Please don't tell me how to drive,' Trish says, flooring the accelerator and zipping from lane to lane. They're headed east, towards the outskirts of town.

'This isn't the way. Where are you going?'

'I know what I'm doing,' Trish says, almost running a red light. 'Oops,' she says sweetly.

'Are you insane?' Claudia looks back at Jailhouse, whose head lolls and droops, jerking up for a second and nodding forward again. 'I don't believe it – she's sleeping. How can she be sleeping?'

Wyclef is singing, 'Someone please call 911....' Trish drums the steering wheel, nodding to the beat.

'If you're trying to scare her you're wasting your time, Trish. She's completely oblivious.'

Trish glances in the rear-view mirror, turns to Claudia and smirks. 'I guess it's just you and me, babe.' They're on a two-lane in an industrial area. When they get to a four-way stop on a steep incline, Trish yanks the parking brake so hard the lever snaps right off. She flings it out the window. 'I don't think we need that,' she says and speeds off through the intersection.

'You're a lunatic!'

'Yep.' Trish narrows her eyes. 'And you of course are absolutely perfect. So fucking self-righteous and perfect. A perfect pain in the ass is what you are. Well, guess what?'

'Watch the road!'

'Some things are out of your control, darling. Way out of your control,' Trish says, looking steadily at Claudia as they drift towards the middle of the road. The driver of an oncoming car honks and gestures furiously. Trish gives him the finger, swerves to avoid him and brakes hard. The car bounces onto the gravel shoulder and jolts to a stop inches away from a ditch. 'Ouch!' Trish says. 'I bit my lip.'

'I hate you,' Claudia gasps, clutching her chest.

Jailhouse, who is passed out on the back seat, gives a sharp snore. A half smile flickers briefly across her face and a trail of drool slides down her chin.

'She's out for the count,' Trish says, starting to giggle. Her shoulders shake as she giggles and whoops hysterically in a manic high-pitched crescendo.

'I hate you so much,' Claudia hisses, 'I could kill you.'

Trish can't stop. She laughs so hard she has to wipe her eyes. 'Oh! Ow ow ow!' she pants, hugging her arms under her rib cage. 'That hurts!'

Claudia clenches her jaw. She wants to slap Trish, hard. She wants to hurt her in the worst way. She wants to throttle her, once and for all. Her lower lip trembles and she shakes with fury and terror and relief. She glares at Trish, raises her hand, but then what else can she do but reach for her sister.

'Home sweet home,' Trish trills as they pull up outside the house.

'Unbelievable, she's still sleeping. She must be totally whacked.'

Claudia leans over the seat and gently prods Jailhouse. 'Wakey wakey.'

'Come on, hurry up,' Trish says. 'I'm desperate to pee.'

When they've gathered their things and are back outside with an overjoyed Henry leaping up between them, Trish tosses Claudia the car key. 'All yours,' she says. 'I need a nap.'

Jailhouse opens the passenger door for Trish. 'Um, when's the baby due?' she asks.

'January 16th.'

'January 16th,' Jailhouse repeats solemnly, nodding.

'I'll call you,' Claudia tells Jailhouse, and starts the engine.

'Okaybyebye,' Jailhouse says. She gives a little fluttery wave.

A couple of blocks away Claudia says, 'How's she going to manage without Iris? She'll be lost.'

'She's lost anyway. She'll manage. We all do,' Trish says. 'Don't rev so high. You need to change gears sooner.' She leans back and closes her eyes. On the highway twenty minutes later she opens them briefly and says, 'Do you realize we've both outlived Mom already? I never thought I'd get to be this old.'

Henry's head is shoved out the partly open window. His ears flap back as he sniffs the wind. Claudia turns the heat up high to counter-act the draft. She's driving fairly fast and enjoying it, comfortable with the feel of the car now, but still nowhere as fast as Trish would be driving. Speed for Trish is mysterious and irresistible as gravity.

'You know the baby's father? It's that guy Troy,' Trish says after a few minutes. 'Remember? Troy? Little goatee?'

'The guy from the band? The what's he, the bass player?'

'Drummer. But it's over.' Trish fumbles for a cigarette then puts it back in the pack. 'I can do this, you know. This thing with the baby? I can do it.'

'Not living in the car, you can't.'

It's already dark out. Claudia watches the headlights on the highway and thinks about their mother (tender as a fawn, and as quick to vanish) and father (what was he thinking, fiddling with a bomb?) and about how it would be to have Trish around all the time, in that tiny apartment, messing stuff up. There are things Claudia doesn't want to know about her sister – how she lives, the bleakness and doubt and disappointment, the ways she degrades herself. But careering along the road, hot air from the vents blasting her face and Henry panting down the back of her neck, she glances at her sister and thinks that this is it, this is her entire world, it's just the two of them, and she feels it like a jab to the heart.

'I'm gonna need a labour coach,' Trish says.

'No problem.'

The car glides to a halt outside Claudia's apartment building. 'Okay,' she says. 'We're home,' but Trish just sits there, staring straight ahead. 'Trish?'

Trish sighs and opens the door. 'God, I'm huge. Come help me out of this car. I swear I think we're gonna need a crane.'

RETURN STROKE

One afternoon during a violent thunderstorm, while my grandmother washed dishes beneath the open kitchen window, lightning
struck and her hands caught fire. She sprang away from the sink and
stood gaping at her blazing hands until Uncle Hank, who had just
come into the kitchen, grabbed a dishtowel and smothered the
flames. 'Oh my,' Grandmother said.

I've invented the 'Oh my,' but she would have said that.

In her frequent retelling of this incident since its occurrence
some thirty-five years ago, Grandmother has said she felt no real
pain – just a quick mild burning sensation in the centres of both
palms, and then a sort of tingling that spread up her arms and
zapped her heart. Well, zapped is my word – she wouldn't say that.

The fire left no outward traces – no weals of scar tissue or
scorched discoloured skin – but soon after she was struck by lightning my grandmother found she had developed a special 'talent': she
was able to dowse. It was as if the lightning had charged atoms in her
body and somehow she was in alignment, in harmony, with the elec-
tromagnetic fields of this planet. She discovered her ability to divine
the day after this incident, when she was clearing the yard of
branches blown down by the storm. She picked up a forked branch
and it dipped down, suddenly and forcefully, right over the septic
tank.

Grandmother stopped dowsing a couple of years ago, but for
more than three decades it was as if her heart, her soul, the entire
constellation of molecules that form her could shrug loose and pierce
the soil; slip through caves and rocks to deposits of metallic ores, or
underground streams.

This became the single most important thing about her, more
momentous than the births or deaths or anything else that had or
would happen in her life: a stroke of lightning had singled her out.

Grandmother lies in a rented hospital bed in Uncle Hank and his wife Ellie's house. On the bedside table are boxes of chocolates, an alarming assortment of pills, and the TV remote. She has no intention of leaving the bed. In the past few months she's lost first a toe, then a foot, and now her leg below the knee, to gangrene. 'I am dying,' she announced when told of the need for the latest amputation, as casually as she might say, 'It's going to rain today.' This was not for dramatic effect, or to elicit sympathy or denials – she merely wanted it acknowledged, up front, so we wouldn't have to skirt around it.

A board-like contraption has been rigged up under the covers to prevent the bedclothes from pressing down on the amputated stump. When the bed is cranked up, she uses the board as a table to play solitaire on, or a few hands of rummy when I visit. Her eyesight has become too weak for reading. She likes me to read the newspaper to her, from cover to cover. She wants to hear headlines, letters to the editor, birth and death notices, reports of business mergers. 'Oh my,' she says of government corruption, and she titters or gasps at scandals, a coy hand covering her mouth. I skip the more disastrous bits – famine, genocide, mayhem – hoping she won't notice. It sounds crazy, but I'm convinced she is abnormally affected by eruptions of violence, evil and tragedy – bad news is dangerous to her.

My grandmother is a rational woman, inclined toward the scientific rather than the metaphysical. She readily submitted to tests that measured changes in skin potential as she moved over subterranean water; she is familiar with studies suggesting possible detector sites in the human body for magnetic fields – the adrenal gland in the kidney region; the pineal gland at the base of the brain; the retinas of the eyes. She draws parallels between the navigational mechanisms of migratory birds and dowsers. She is adamant in her refusal to believe that what happened to her was a miracle – she will not be allied with paintings that wink or shed tears of blood. She has accepted her talent with the same matter-of-fact resignation she would have shown had she been born cross-eyed, or with twelve toes, or if she'd developed Tourette's syndrome.

I spent a fair amount of time with my grandmother while I was growing up, after my father died and my mother started dating again. I've watched her body react to hidden signals. I've been with her while she stood transformed, her atoms spinning in an irresistible dance with something beneath the surface.

Grandmother observed certain rituals when she dowsed. First she'd wash her hands in hot water, then take a few swigs of whisky-laced tea from the flask she kept with her. She has always suffered from poor circulation – blood moves sluggishly around her rotund body to her extremities – but she dowsed without gloves, even in cold weather, so she could feel the rod against her skin. Her fingers would be raw, numb with cold, yet the centres of her palms tingled as if their contact with the dowsing rod had reignited molecular memories of the lightning bolt. She favoured a Y-stick cut from a willow. She'd stride off across fields in her thick cardigan and muddy boots, a woollen tuque pulled down over her ears, brandishing the Y-stick like a tilted crucifix and moving as quickly as her short stout legs would allow. 'The faster I move,' she'd say, 'the stronger the reaction.'

These strong reactions were taxing – Grandmother has described the sensations as akin to a series of electric shocks sweeping across her body. She'd tremble with the chills; her teeth would chatter; fear would lurch and somersault in her stomach.

'Have another chocolate, go on,' she says. 'Do you know, even the police used me, to find bodies?'

I nod. 'I remember.' I was there, for the first body. Well, not exactly *there*, out with her when she found it, but I was there afterwards, when she came home. That was the summer my mother remarried, when I was fourteen.

'Nowadays they've got radar that can scan underground,' she says. 'I saw it on the television. They used it in the backyard of that horrible man – the one who kidnapped those children and took such dreadful photographs of them. But all they found buried in his garden were old cow bones.'

'I wish you wouldn't watch stuff like that,' I say.

'Not that I'd be much good any more – they'd have to drag me around in a wheelchair. Now that would be a sight – imagine me bumping around out there, dangling my foot over scrub and mud. Go on, take another chocolate. Take a few.'

Finding the first body was an accident. Grandmother had been hired by a construction company to dowse for hidden service lines on a long-abandoned site near the outskirts of town. As she tramped over some muddy soil beneath a clump of trees, her Y-stick twisted so violently the bark ripped off and tore the skin on her hands. When labourers from the construction company dug, they found the battered body of young Shannon Peterson. She'd been missing for three weeks, last seen leaving for softball practice at a park a few blocks from her home.

The gruesome discovery caused my grandmother to feel as if she'd arrived at the end of something; as if she'd slipped through the safety net of the world and was falling headlong, mouth open. This was the dark side of the gift – a startling, almost unknowable sorrow pulsed outward from her heart.

After this she began to move more cautiously over the earth, waiting for another shock or a fissure that might open up and swallow her. She pushed the terror deep inside and held it there. It has congealed into something wobbly and gelatinous – a bright, throbbing clot.

'While you're here, would you mind helping me bathe her?'

Aunt Ellie fills an enamel basin with warm water, and hands me towels and soap.

'She hates this,' Aunt Ellie warns. 'She's as bashful as a young girl. But better you than Hank.'

We roll my grandmother onto her side, remove her nightgown, and slide a towel under her. She moans, and closes her watery eyes. I try not to look at the remains of her leg, the exposed stump. Aunt Ellie washes her face and neck, soaps her belly, the pink folds between her legs, her empty flapping breasts. We help her to sit upright. 'Oh!' she whispers, and her lips contract, bluish, around the sound. I hold her while Aunt Ellie washes her back. Her crimped skin feels cold and loose. Aunt Ellie pats her dry, sprinkles her with powder, and we help her into a clean nightgown.

'You smell nice,' I tell her as I comb her hair. She keeps it bobbed short, parted on one side. It's hardly greying, but beginning to thin. Strands of hair fall and coil like dark pencilled arcs on her pillow. Specks of talcum powder and tiny flakes of skin fleck the pale blue sheets.

Ever since the lightning struck, atmospheric changes have affected Grandmother – the altitude and position of the sun; the strength and direction of the wind; the approach of storms. It was fine when she was doing run-of-the-mill dowsing for wells and tree roots, but once she began to look for bodies, her acute sensitivity extended beyond mere weather conditions. Now even distant events affect her. Misery blows through her, and as the television brings news of war, earthquakes, mutilations, her condition worsens.

I discuss this with Uncle Hank and Aunt Ellie. 'You ought to install some sort of V-chip in that thing,' I tell them. 'Look how it's affecting her. She's disintegrating.'

They exchange frowns.

Uncle Hank speaks carefully. 'Any doctor will tell you – and she'd be the first to agree – there are perfectly reasonable explanations for her condition.'

I know. Poor circulation, immobility, ulcerated flesh, putrefaction, amputation. Infection, amputation. And so on. Vision clouded – age-related. The bedridden have feelings of morbidity. These things happen.

But they cannot deny she has developed a highly unusual sensitivity to the world. Images of massacres in Algeria flicker across the TV screen, and my grandmother's limbs ache. Flood victims weep and her head throbs.

'Listen, dear,' Aunt Ellie says gently, 'it's not good for you to be cooped up with an invalid. You're young. You should be out with people your own age.'

'Your grandmother loves that TV,' Uncle Hank says. 'She likes to keep informed. Her mind's still sharp as a tack.'

Grim self-sacrifice pinches the corners of Aunt Ellie's mouth. 'Don't get me wrong – we love having you visit, but now's the time to be enjoying your life.'

'But I'm *happy* to be here,' I protest, and leave the rest unsaid – *besides, she won't be around much longer.*

I do have a life beyond my deteriorating grandmother, and my aunt and uncle who've become impatient and exhausted from the demands of nursing her. I spend hours surrounded by – and in various degrees of contact with – strong, lithe, breathtakingly mobile bodies. We engage in tugs-of-war with gravity; we tease the limits of skin, muscle and air.

Alex could have used that in his documentary about me – tugs-of-war with gravity; teasing limits – although he probably would have said it was over-the-top. *Let your choreography speak for itself. Your dancing is so eloquent, you don't need words.*

I lived with Alex for almost two years. He took rolls of footage of me at rehearsals, on tour, in the park, shopping, cooking – Alex and his camera were everywhere. He had enormous energy – he hardly slept. If he wasn't filming or editing, he'd be baking bread, or taking his motorbike apart, or painting the walls, or speeding down the highway, or calling everyone he knew.

The final argument took place after he'd woken me at 3:00 a.m. to tell me the lighting designer was undermining my work with subliminal messages, and I had to get rid of him. A week earlier it had been one of the musicians.

'It's no good,' I said. 'I can't do this any more.'

When I came home from rehearsals that evening, I found Alex lying on his back on the futon with a clear plastic bag over his head, held tight around his neck with elastic bands. Beside the futon were a bottle of tequila and an empty pill container. The new Counting Crows was playing – we'd listened to it for the first time late one night that week with the lights out – but six discs were loaded in the magazine of the CD player. At the moment of his death, Alex could have heard the Brahms Violin Concerto, Tom Waits, Big Audio Dynamite, Cecilia Bartoli, or Ali Farka Toure.

There was no suicide note, but on the kitchen counter was a photograph he'd taken of me a few months earlier at a sidewalk sale – I'd tried on a pair of outrageous cat's-eye sunglasses with fluorescent orange frames. Alex had cropped the photograph and mounted it on a sheet of rose-coloured cardboard. Diagonally across the cardboard he'd written: *last seen enjoying her illusions.*

That happened eight months ago. The aftershocks are unavoidable. All it takes is the scent of a particular shaving soap, or an inadvertent envelope addressed to the dead, shoved through the mail slot with bills and flyers and a card from Mother, or some music first heard late with the lights out, and the ground threatens to break open.

In her dreams, my grandmother is falling. She jerks as she sleeps; little spasms shake her like jolts of electricity.

There is something about me that Grandmother and Uncle Hank and Aunt Ellie wouldn't want to know, although it's actually quite harmless, and perfectly safe. For the past few months I've been supplementing my income with phone sex. I have the perfect voice, and it's easy, once you get the hang of it. You can chop celery or sort laundry or do some basic stretches while they're jerking off on the other end of the line. You just have to remember to talk dirty from time to time – it's not hard to figure out what they want – and to keep moaning and breathing heavily. Most of my clients are repeats. Some want to meet me, but of course that's out of the question.

A man is setting up a telescope on the sidewalk diagonally opposite

Uncle Hank and Aunt Ellie's house. It's an unusually cold night for the beginning of spring.

Grandmother watches news of oil spills, refugees, nuclear leaks, bombings. A female torso with surgically severed limbs stuffed in a bag near a railway line. Cult suicides, comet madness.

I turn off the TV. 'Come outside with me. I want you to see the comet.'

'I can't, dear,' she says.

'It's perfect tonight – no clouds. There's a guy out there with a telescope. Come.'

Uncle Hank helps me lift her into the wheelchair. We put a couple of thick socks on her foot, tuck blankets around her, muffle her with scarf and hat and gloves.

I push her slowly down the front walk and steer her over to the man fiddling with his telescope. He looks quite young. He's wearing a beret and a leather jacket with the collar pulled up over his neck.

'Hi,' I say. 'Mind if we take a look through your telescope?'

'Sorry. I can't get the comet in focus. My hands are shaking too much – it's so cold.' He speaks with an accent I can't place. 'It's a delicate instrument.'

'What a shame,' Grandmother says.

'You can see without the telescope,' and he points to it – clear and bright, its tail streaming upwards.

'My grandmother's eyesight's not good,' I explain.

'Then we'll have to keep trying.' He lowers the stand, crouches down, repositions the angle of the telescope, blows on his hands and rubs them together, makes minute adjustments to the eyepiece. 'Okay,' he says after a few minutes. 'I have it.' Little fires of exhilaration dance in his black eyes.

We manoeuvre the wheelchair so that Grandmother can have a look.

'Oh my – how wonderful!' she exclaims.

When I take my turn at the telescope, Grandmother says, 'I've heard that every carbon atom inside each one of us comes from some distant star.' After a few moments, she adds, 'My granddaughter here is a dancer.' She is gazing up, apparently transfixed by the vast, spinning night sky.

I laugh. 'My grandmother here has a remarkable ability to navigate.'

Aunt Ellie brings cups of hot tea after we get Grandmother back to bed.

'Perhaps that young man out there would like some tea to warm him up. I'd like a drop of whisky in mine, Ellie, for a nightcap. It was terribly cold outside.'

'That'll be the day – not with all the medication you're taking,' Aunt Ellie says. 'You should rest when you finish your tea. Be sure you don't overdo it.'

'Good heavens, I'll have more than enough rest when I'm dead. If I had both legs, I'd go dancing.' After Aunt Ellie has gone, she sighs and pats my hand. 'A daughter-in-law is not the same as a daughter.'

'Your hands feel warm tonight,' I say. There are small clusters of blister-like eruptions in the centres of both palms. 'How long have you had this rash?'

'I hadn't noticed. It must be a reaction to all these pills.' She sips her tea and pulls a face. 'Want to play a few hands of rummy before you go?'

I shuffle the cards.

'Remember how my hands caught fire, in a lightning storm?' she says. 'Well, of course you couldn't *remember*, you weren't born yet. You know, lightning isn't just one single stroke that falls to earth and then that's over and done with. There's some give-and-take involved.'

I begin to deal the cards. 'What do you mean?'

'Well, apparently the thundercloud sends down negative charges, but before they reach the ground, opposite charges from houses or trees – or my soapy hands, for that matter – rush to meet them somewhere up there. You see, there's mutual attraction.' She picks up her cards, sorts them. 'All that energy and fury – the flash of light, the thunder – is really from what they call the return stroke, which goes back up to the cloud. It moves so quickly, we can't see it's actually rising, not falling.' She picks up a card from the top of the pack and smiles.

I lower her bed, smooth the sheets, kiss her forehead. 'So,' Grandmother says, and blinks. Her eyes say the rest – *I am dying. Have another chocolate. Take two. Go on.*

When I close my eyes she is there, an after-image on the retinas.

My grandmother taught me never to bathe or use electric appliances during a thunderstorm. I will hang up the phone when there's lightning, even if my client is in the final throes of passion. If I'm caught outside in an electrical storm, I know not to shelter under a tree. I'll look for the lowest point and crouch, keeping both feet on the ground.

ACKNOWLEDGMENTS

Grateful acknowledgment is made to the journals and anthologies in which these stories, or slightly different versions of them, were previously published: 'Anything that Wiggles' appeared in *Prairie Fire* and also in *The Journey Prize Anthology 13* (McClelland & Stewart, 2001); 'The Bending Moments of Beams' was published in *PRISM international*; 'Colleen, through the Window' was published in *TickleAce*; 'Detour' appeared in *Coming Attractions: 00* (Oberon, 2000); 'Lorna Gets a Tattoo' was published in *Dandelion*; 'Most Wanted' was published in *The New Quarterly*; 'Orange Buoys' was published in *Grain*; 'Return Stroke' appeared in *The Capilano Review* and also in *Coming Attractions: 00* (Oberon, 2000); 'Smile on Mrs G' was published in *Pottersfield Portfolio*; 'Soft Spot' appeared in *The Malahat Review* and also in *Coming Attractions: 00* (Oberon, 2000).

Acknowledgment is also made for the use of excerpts from 'Little Sister'. Words and Music by Doc Pomus and Mort Shuman. Copyright © 1961 by Elvis Presley Music, Inc. Copyright Renewed and Assigned to Elvis Presley Music. All Rights Administered by Cherry River Music Co. and Chrysalis Songs. International Copyright Secured. All Rights Reserved.

I am especially grateful to my editor, John Metcalf, for his invaluable guidance and support, and to Tim and Elke Inkster and intern Jack Illingworth at The Porcupine's Quill. My sincere thanks to the editors of the various publications in which these stories first appeared, especially Maggie Helwig. Thanks to John Grube for early encouragement and to Anne Montagnes for criticism and sage advice. I am immensely grateful to the members of the Phoebe-Walmer Collective (Suzanne Collins, Laura Lush, Jim Nason and Eddy Yanofsky) for their unfailing generosity in sharing their time and talents, and for their indispensable wisdom and wit regarding matters writerly and otherwise. I am also grateful to Nadia Habib and Elisavietta Ritchie for long-standing support, encouragement and editorial input. My thanks to all my friends who bear with me and cheer me on, despite my tendency to pilfer snippets of their lives shamelessly. And of course my immeasurable thanks to Moss and Ruby and my mother, for everything.

Vivette J. Kady grew up in South Africa where she studied architecture before immigrating to Canada and starting to write. She now lives in Toronto. Her fiction has appeared in numerous journals and anthologies in Canada and the United States, including *The Journey Prize Anthology*, *Coming Attractions* and *Best Canadian Stories*, and has been shortlisted for the Journey Prize, a National Magazine Award and a Western Magazine Award.